SECRETS OF THE CASTLETON MANOR LIBRARY

On Pens and Needles

Sandra Orchard

Annie's
AnniesFiction.com

Books in the Secrets of the Castleton Manor Library series

Library of Congress-in-Publication Data
On Pens and Needles / by Sandra Orchard
p. cm.
I. Title
2018935311

AnniesFiction.com
(800) 282-6643
Secrets of the Castleton Manor Library™
Series Creator: Shari Lohner
Series Editor: Lorie Jones
Cover Illustrator: Jesse Reisch

10 11 12 13 14 | Printed in South Korea | 9 8 7 6 5 4

"Why do people forward chain letters?" Faith Newberry, Castleton Manor's librarian, deleted the e-mail from Carrie, their newest housekeeper.

Faith's black-and-white tuxedo cat, Watson, who'd been staring at the computer from his perch on the corner of the library's expansive desk, emitted a wary yowl.

"Nothing bad is going to happen," Faith told him. "I'm not superstitious."

"Not at all?" Carrie appeared from behind a nearby bookcase, feather duster in hand. She sounded as if the concept of someone not being superstitious was beyond comprehension.

"Not at all," Faith said firmly. "People who start these e-mails are not doing you any favors. They promise you prosperity if you pass it along and bad luck if you break the chain. The letter merely manipulates you into altering your perspective."

"What do you mean?"

"Say I stub my toe. If I didn't break the e-mail's chain, I wouldn't think it was bad luck, just something that happened. But if I failed to follow the instructions, I might start thinking every little bad thing that happened to me was because I broke the chain, right?"

Carrie shrugged. "Maybe it is."

Faith sighed. Apparently, sound reasoning wasn't going to curb the young woman's superstitions. "Did you send one to Ms. Russell?"

Carrie bit her bottom lip. "No. Do you think I should have?"

"That would be the fastest way to lose your job," Faith said. "Which wouldn't help in the prosperity department." Marlene Russell, the manor's assistant manager, was all business and might have fired

Carrie on the spot for gleaning employee e-mail addresses from the staff notices and using them for correspondence that wasn't related to work. "You didn't send this to any guests, did you?"

Carrie shook her head, her bottom lip trembling now.

"Good. Ms. Russell wouldn't appreciate staff using the private e-mail addresses guests entrust us with for anything other than Castleton Manor business."

Carrie twisted the feather duster's handle nervously. "I was only trying to help people."

Faith softened her tone, regretting how sharply she'd spoken. "I know your heart was in the right place. But e-mails like these should be confined to your personal, not professional, acquaintances. Okay?"

"Yes. I'm sorry. I didn't mean to upset anyone."

Faith offered her a reassuring smile. "I'm afraid the theme of this upcoming retreat already has me a little on edge."

The four-day event was hosted by a group of horror writers. The goal was to provide aspiring writers and fans an opportunity to connect with authors and learn more about the horror genre through panel discussions and social events.

Carrie's eyes widened. "You don't like horror novels?"

"No. I don't like to be frightened." Faith imagined the horror group would make the events as creepy as possible. She shuddered. Being scared out of her wits was not her idea of a good time.

"Oh, I love horror," Carrie gushed. "Novels. Movies. Short stories."

It was Faith's turn to be surprised. If she were as superstitious as the young woman, she'd avoid the genre altogether. "Why?"

Carrie grinned, her eyes gleaming. "It's a great excuse to let your emotions go without anyone thinking you're crazy."

"I guess that's true." Except for the people who thought Carrie was crazy to want to watch or read it in the first place. But Faith kept that thought to herself.

"Aren't you finished in here yet?" Marlene barked at Carrie from the doorway. "They need help setting out refreshments in the Main Hall for arriving guests."

"Sorry. Yes, I'll go right now." Carrie streaked out of the library as if her feather duster were on fire.

Marlene smoothed a strand of blonde hair that had escaped the bun at the nape of her neck. "Why do all the young housekeepers have to be so inept?"

Faith chuckled. "They just seem that way because you make them nervous."

"If they can't take active supervision, they don't belong here," Marlene snapped. Her gaze flitted over the display Faith had set up to showcase books written by the authors participating in the retreat.

Marlene picked up a copy of *Superstition: A Collection of Short Stories*, the newest release of the retreat's star attraction, Pierce Baltimore. "Good idea putting Mr. Baltimore's books front and center. I've heard he has a bit of an ego."

"It seemed fitting."

Marlene's attention drifted to Watson still sitting on Faith's desk, and her countenance darkened.

Faith thought it was strange that the assistant manager of the pet-friendly resort was not fond of animals. Fortunately, Marlene had begun to grudgingly accept Watson's presence in the manor.

"Are you all prepared for your lecture tomorrow?" Marlene asked.

Faith shut off her computer and gathered her papers into a file folder. "Yes, I'm focusing on classic horror." They were the only books she'd dared sample.

"I'm sure that will be fine. Why don't you go mingle with the guests now?"

Faith hesitated. She was usually more than happy to chat with guests, but because she didn't share this group's appreciation of horror, she feared she'd be put on the spot and feel uncomfortable.

"Is there a problem?" Marlene pointedly checked her watch.

"No, there's no problem."

"Good." Marlene strode toward the door, her heels clicking a brisk staccato on the floor. She glanced over her shoulder. "Don't dawdle."

Watson jumped down from Faith's desk, strolled over to the terrace door, and meowed.

"You're not interested in mixing with vampires and werewolves either? I don't blame you." Faith opened the door for him and shivered. The autumn air had grown chilly, and fallen leaves swirled around the grounds. "Now don't get into any mischief. I'll be home in a couple of hours."

Watson arched his back, his tail—shortened to a stub in an accident when he was a kitten—poking straight up. Then he strolled outside.

Who was she kidding? He never listened to her.

Faith locked the terrace door, slipped her file folder into her bag, and flicked off the lights on her way out the door that opened into the gallery. Voices carried through the long, marbled room that stretched two stories high and offered breathtaking ocean views. She paused to take in the scenery, hoping it would calm her nerves.

Instead, she spotted an apparition out of the corner of her eye and couldn't help but jump, even though she knew it wasn't real.

She peered at it more closely. Someone had fashioned thin chicken wire into the shape of a life-size person who appeared to be sneaking a peek around one of the pillars. Painted white, it looked ethereally real. Faith had to admit she was impressed by the retreat organizer's creativity, even if the horror-themed decoration had utterly undone the ocean view's calming effect.

Turning back to the window, Faith glimpsed a hand sticking out of one of the large flowerpots, a forked trowel gripped in its fist.

Releasing a sigh, she meandered toward the reception area, being careful to avoid the all-too-realistic spiderwebs spanning the short distances from statues to pillars and gracing the corners of several paintings. She was surprised that Wolfe Jaxon, co-owner of Castleton

Manor, had allowed those decorations considering how old and valuable some of the paintings were.

Of course, maybe he didn't know. In addition to overseeing the retreats at the manor, he ran his family's various businesses. He was often away from the estate for days or even weeks at a time. And she hadn't seen him around in the last few days.

Faith peered more closely at the spiderwebs to make sure the decorations hadn't stuck to the paintings' surfaces.

"There you are." Marlene caught Faith by the elbow, her sparking green eyes softening with something akin to relief. She guided Faith over to a clearly distraught blonde hugging a huge black cat.

The woman appeared to be in her early thirties and perfectly normal—no dark scary makeup, no blood-smeared clothing, no prongs sticking out of her neck, no fangs in her mouth. Faith glanced around and breathed a happy sigh, glad that none of the other guests had elected to dress in thematic costumes as other retreat attendees tended to do.

"This is Miss Tara Blue," Marlene told Faith. "She's waiting for Dr. Foster to arrive. Since you like cats, I thought you might keep her company until then."

Faith smiled and introduced herself to Tara.

"Please excuse me," Marlene said abruptly, then pivoted on her heel and walked away.

Faith gave the cat an affectionate scratch behind the ears. "What's wrong with your little fellow?"

"She's a girl. Midnight's diabetic. I was sure I packed her insulin and syringes, but they're not here. I don't know what happened." Tara's voice rose in panic with each sentence.

"Don't worry," Faith reassured her. "Midge—that's Dr. Foster—is wonderful. She'll take good care of Midnight and stock you with whatever she needs." Midge Foster was the manor's concierge vet and one of Faith's good friends.

"Do you have a cat?"

"Yes. His name is Watson, and he comes to work with me in the library. He just went outside. Perhaps Midnight will get a chance to meet him."

Tara smiled, her panic appearing to abate. "It's amazing that they let us bring our pets into such an elegant place. I'd be petrified the cats would scratch the pillars or that statue of Agatha Christie or something."

Faith chuckled. "The pillars are all marble. I'm pretty sure a cat couldn't hurt them." Faith spotted Midge wading through the lobby with her vet bag, an unfamiliar man at her side. Faith waved her over and said to Tara, "Here comes our vet now. If you get an opportunity to go into town, be sure to stop at Midge's Happy Tails Gourmet Bakery. It has the most amazing treats for pets."

"Did you hear that?" Tara whispered to her cat, then looked sheepishly at Faith. "I'm afraid I give Midnight more treats than I probably should."

"Midge's recipes are very healthy since she's a vet. Watson especially loves the tunaroons," Faith said.

Midge strode up to them and grinned at Midnight. "This beautiful girl must be my patient," she said. "What seems to be the trouble?"

Tara quickly explained her dilemma.

Faith could see that she, like most people, visibly relaxed on meeting the comforting, clearly capable Midge.

"That's not a problem," Midge said. "Let's go to the pet spa, where Bill and I can examine her properly, and then we'll see about getting you a supply of insulin and syringes."

Faith extended her hand to Bill, who'd been standing quietly nearby, studying Midnight and her owner. "I'm Faith."

He shook her hand. "Bill. Pleased to meet you."

"Oh, I'm sorry," Midge added. "I should have made the introductions. Bill is a vet from Martha's Vineyard."

"I'm thinking about starting a concierge service for some of the resorts there," Bill said in a baritone radio voice that no doubt lulled his patients' human parents into as calm a state as it did their pets. "Midge kindly invited me to spend a few days shadowing her here so I could see firsthand how she makes it work."

"Ah, so we'll be seeing you around," Faith said as they wound through the mingling guests to reach the pet spa at the far end of the manor.

"Marlene says quite a few guests brought pets this week, so you might," Midge said. "We'll be at the stables for sure. One of the horses is expecting a foal any day now."

"Wow, this place has everything," Tara said.

"We aim to please," Faith said with a smile.

They entered the spa, and Midge led the way to a private room. Tara set Midnight on the table.

Bill handled the exam, and his dulcet tones immediately settled the quivering feline. "You're a reporter, aren't you?" he asked Tara.

"Yes, how did you know?"

"I recognize your name and face from the magazine. So what brings you here?"

She blushed. "Secretly, I hope to become a novelist. Officially, I'm here to cover the event for the magazine."

"A novelist, huh?" Bill said. "I've heard it can be hard to break into publishing."

"It can be. Yes."

"But I imagine your well-written interviews will have won you the gratitude of more than a few successful authors," Bill said. "Perhaps enough for them to put in a good word about you to their agent or publisher?"

Tara grinned. "Maybe one day. So far I've only written short stories. But I want to start a horror novel."

"Well, you should find plenty of fodder for a killer story among a group of horror writers," Bill remarked.

"I sure hope so."

Watching from the sidelines, Faith said, "I have to say I prefer my reading material a little more sedate. What made you decide to write horror?"

"They say to write what you enjoy reading," Tara answered. "And I became hooked on horror novels the first time I read a Pierce Baltimore book."

Midnight squirmed in Bill's hold as he reached for the needle.

"Here, let me take care of the injection," Midge said, moving in beside Bill at the table. She deftly administered the insulin while keeping up a cheery dialogue about how reading Dr. Herriot's books about his years as a country vet in Yorkshire, England, had inspired her to become a vet.

Midge packed up ten syringes and a vial of insulin to get Midnight through the retreat and handed the bag to Tara.

"Thank you, Dr. Foster." Tara glanced over Midge's shoulder. "And, Doctor . . . ?

"Just call me Bill."

"Thanks." Tara picked up Midnight, cuddled her close, and walked out.

Midge closed the door behind her. "That went well. Guests always appreciate it when we take an interest in their occupations or hobbies."

"I read a lot," Bill replied.

"That's good," Midge said. "It'll give you a broad knowledge base to draw from."

Pounding erupted on the door, and then Tara burst in. "A dog coming out of the spa spooked Midnight, and she jumped out of my arms and ran away. Now I can't find her."

"We'll help," Faith offered. "She couldn't have gotten far. And I know Watson's favorite places to hide."

They all dashed out of the pet spa.

Another staff member pointed to the nearby staircase. "If you're looking for the black cat, it ran down to the basement."

"Thanks!" Faith raced down, leading the way.

A bloodcurdling scream drew them toward the laundry room.

Carrie stood in the doorway, her palm splayed across her chest, her face pale. "A b-black cat just crossed my path," she stammered. "That's not good. Not good at all."

"Which way did she run?" Faith asked as Midge and Bill peeked into each room off the hallway.

Carrie pointed a shaky finger toward the kitchen.

Faith started that way, then glanced over her shoulder and noticed Tara wasn't following her. Instead, the reporter was rooted to the spot, studying Carrie with a peculiar expression. "Are you coming?" Faith called to her.

Faith's words seemed to jolt the other woman, and she hurried after Faith. "Do you know the housekeeper's name?" she asked Faith when she slowed outside the kitchen door.

"That was Carrie."

"The woman who screamed? Her name is Carrie?"

"Yes. Why?"

Tara frowned. "I thought I recognized her. She reminds me of a writer I met at some meetings a while back. But it's not her. The name's different."

Brooke Milner, the manor's sous-chef, stepped out of the kitchen with Midnight in her arms. "Are you looking for this gorgeous kitty?"

Tara took Midnight from Brooke. "You naughty girl. You aren't allowed to run away." Tara thanked Brooke profusely, then headed upstairs to settle the cat in her room.

Faith alerted Midge and Bill that the cat had been found, and the two vets went upstairs too.

Faith lingered in the kitchen to chat with her friend.

Brooke gave her the once-over. "You don't look so good." She shed her apron and pulled on a clean one. "Do you still have the heebie-jeebies about this retreat?"

Brooke and Faith, along with Midge and Faith's aunt Eileen Piper, were all part of the Candle House Book Club. At their last meeting, Faith had confided that she felt unusually edgy about the theme for this week's retreat.

Faith tried to shake out the tension in her shoulders. "I know it sounds crazy, but I just can't get over this sense of foreboding. It makes me feel so anxious. This is why I don't read horror."

"Yeah, I understand. You know I prefer romance," Brooke said. "I guess we should be happy they didn't schedule the retreat over Halloween."

"I don't know. Friday is the thirteenth. One guess what movie they'll show that night." Faith made a sour face.

Brooke laughed. "You'll be enjoying a warm cup of tea, snuggled up with Watson in front of the fireplace at your cottage by then."

"So true."

Brooke pulled a tray of deviled eggs and a jar of black olives from the fridge. "Have you heard about Pierce Baltimore's new book? I had no idea how many superstitions there were out there."

"I glanced through a few of the stories. I really prefer not to read horror."

"How about chain letters?" Brooke set to work slicing olives. "Did you get one from Carrie?"

Faith rolled her eyes. "Yes, and I told her not to send such things to staff again. She's lucky she didn't include Marlene."

"I take it you didn't forward it to ten friends."

"No way. You didn't, did you?"

Brooke shrugged. She set half an olive upside down on top of a deviled egg and arranged additional slivers around it, like spider legs. "I figured it couldn't hurt."

Faith gaped at her. "You don't believe all that stuff in the letter, do you?"

"No."

"So why inflict it on ten friends when it's bound to irritate them?"

Brooke grinned. "I sent it to former colleagues and cooking school classmates who have annoyed me."

Faith laughed as she shook her head. "You're terrible."

Another cook in the kitchen groaned. "Maybe I shouldn't have deleted mine." She showed them a giant hole in the loaf of bread she was cutting.

"Oh yeah, that's not good," Brooke said.

"That hole didn't happen because she deleted the chain letter," Faith argued. "It probably would have happened anyway. It's not bad luck."

"No," Brooke said. "A hole in a loaf of bread means someone is going to die."

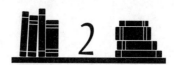

The next morning, Faith grimaced at the dark circles under her eyes as she combed her hair. She'd slept fitfully, thanks to dreams about bread with holes, black cats walking under ladders, and an in-box overflowing with chain letters.

"I'll be so glad when this retreat is over," she said to Watson.

He gave her his indignant my-food-dish-is-still-empty meow.

Faith laughed. "Thanks for the show of solidarity." She tossed her comb onto the counter. "Come on. Let's have breakfast."

The sun shone through the cottage windows, lightening Faith's mood but not enough to get more than three bites of toast down. Butterflies were having a heyday in her stomach. Judging by how Watson was wolfing down his kibble, he wasn't having the same problem.

This was crazy. She rarely got this nervous about a presentation. Was she worried the guests would see right through her? Figure out how little she knew about the genre they clearly loved?

She glanced at the clock and jumped to her feet. The lecture was due to start in twenty minutes. She quickly brushed her teeth and took one more swipe at her hair, which she'd left hanging around her shoulders, then grabbed her bag. "You coming?" she asked Watson.

The cat inspected his again-empty bowl one last time, then sauntered toward the front door.

Halfway between the cottage and the manor, Watson peeled off, apparently in search of something more interesting than her lecture on classic horror.

Faith cut through the historic Victorian garden and stopped short at the sound of a heated argument. But she didn't stop soon enough to avoid interrupting the pair standing between the foxglove and the fountain grass.

Tara clutched Midnight to her chest while a dark-haired man towered over her. Faith recognized the author Pierce Baltimore from the photo on his dust jackets.

Pierce glowered at Tara before transforming his expression into a pleasant smile and nodding to Faith.

"Good morning," Faith said, giving them a smile of her own. "Tara, I wanted to ask you about something. Would you walk with me?"

Tara hurried toward her.

Faith made up some small talk until they were out of earshot of Pierce. Glancing over her shoulder, Faith saw him stalking off in the direction of the kennels. "Are you all right?" she asked Tara.

The woman nodded. "Thank you," she said, her voice shaking. As they reached the terrace, Tara turned and darted off toward the topiaries before Faith could say another word.

She probably wanted to be alone to collect herself after what had looked like a rather frightening experience. And Faith needed to get to the library. She slipped inside the manor.

By the time she reached the library, a small crowd had already gathered outside the door. Their gasps as Faith welcomed them in had nothing to do with horror decorations. A skeleton doormat outside the library's entrance was as close as the retreat organizer had been able to get to Faith's domain.

Faith smiled, despite her dread of giving a lecture in the next hour on a subject she preferred to avoid. The walnut-paneled, two-story room brimming with books of all kinds, some more than 150 years old, still filled her with awe too.

Someone had already gotten a fire going in the fireplace to take the nip out of the air. So Faith treated the early arrivals to a brief tour of the library's main sections. Of course, everyone was most interested in the handful of rare horror classics. The first editions were enclosed in the locked glass bookcases.

Faith donned a pair of white cotton gloves and removed Mary

Shelley's *Frankenstein* from the case. "Published in 1818, this classic Gothic novel is arguably one of the most influential works of the modern horror genre, and it is the main one I will be talking about today."

Enthusiastic murmurs rippled through the group gathered around the book.

Faith glanced at the newcomers trickling into the room and then at the clock. "I guess I'd better put this away now. It's that time."

A petite redhead strode into the room and approached Faith with a smile. "I'm Cybil Crypt, the organizer of the retreat." She extended her hand.

Faith shook the woman's hand and introduced herself. "Welcome to Castleton. Please let me know if there's anything you need."

"Thank you." Cybil surveyed the three rows of chairs that had been arranged in the open space near the massive fireplace. "Everything looks good. Let's get started." She went to the front of the room and asked the stragglers to find a seat, then introduced Faith.

Faith took Cybil's place and scanned the crowd. She noticed that Pierce sat in the back row nearest the bookcases, his gaze fixed on Tara, who was in front on the opposite side. The way he focused on Tara piqued Faith's curiosity, and she wondered what their earlier disagreement had been about. She chided herself that it was none of her business, then brushed the thought aside and focused on her notes.

Faith began by sharing background information on the works of Edgar Allan Poe and some of the more prominent early horror novels such as Oscar Wilde's *The Picture of Dorian Gray*, Bram Stoker's *Dracula*, and Robert Louis Stevenson's *The Strange Case of Dr. Jekyll and Mr. Hyde*.

"Although mankind has likely tried to terrify each other with tales for as long as we've told stories," Faith said, "Mary Shelley is the best known author of the earliest novels in the horror genre. Two hundred years ago she wrote *Frankenstein*. It came about when she was having a literary discussion with a group of friends and one of them—Lord Byron, actually—suggested that they all write a horror story.

"As other scholars have noted through the years, Mary's unfortunate family circumstances most likely had a tremendous influence on her story. Her mother died shortly after Mary was born. And the novel's foundation is that of a creator so dismayed by the creature he's made that he abandons it."

As she evaluated a book's merits from a scholar's point of view—by assessing its themes and ability to evoke emotion in the reader—she had to acknowledge how creative and well written many of the enduring horror novels were. But she still didn't like being frightened in order to appreciate a story.

"I believe the reason *Frankenstein* has retained its hold on our imaginations for two centuries is because it delves into some of our most fundamental fears. Monsters aren't just deformed creatures. They are serial killers and abusers. And every one of those monsters has parents who may wish to disown him."

Several in the audience nodded.

"The novel also grips us with its range of implications," Faith went on. "For example, who defines a monster? What is the responsibility of parents to their children? Should society be held accountable for people's rage when it fails to offer them compassion and care? And the list goes on."

Cybil raised her hand. "I noticed that the library's first edition of *Frankenstein* doesn't give the author's name. Why do you suppose the publisher did that?"

"That's a very good question," Faith responded, though she didn't know how to answer it properly. "It wasn't until the second edition was published that Mary Shelley's name appeared on the cover. And of course her name appears on what has become the most popular and widely read version that was published in 1831. That edition went through extensive revisions to tone down the original version's more radical ideas." Or so Faith had read in her research.

"But isn't it true," Cybil pressed, "that the publisher presumed it would not sell as well if it had a woman's name on the cover?"

Faith's eyes widened at the vehemence in Cybil's tone. "I suspect the publisher was more concerned about protecting her from criticism, because everyone had to realize that many readers would find the entire tale disgusting. As we know, this proved to be true."

Cybil snorted. "Mary Shelley faced the same bias against women that we face today. If a man's name is on the cover, critics take it more seriously and publishers put more money behind it to market it." She gestured to Pierce. "My novels are every bit as good as Baltimore's, but the reality is our publisher puts twice as much money into showcasing the books of their male authors. So it's not surprising that they should become the best sellers ahead of other—perhaps even better—novels."

Faith cringed, remembering how she had given Pierce's novels the prime position in her display for the retreat. She was certain Cybil had noticed. "I'm afraid I'm far from an expert on the marketing strategies of publishers."

"Anyone with two eyes can see that's what they're doing," Cybil insisted.

"That's probably a topic better addressed in a panel of industry professionals," Faith said, then smiled at the rest of the group. "Any questions about Mary Shelley or—"

Movement at the back of the room caught Faith's attention, and on the pretext of waiting for a question, she paced to the side aisle. Then she noticed the bookcase behind Pierce start to teeter.

Faith sprinted past the rows of chairs. "Watch out!" She pushed Pierce out of harm's way just as the bookcase toppled, catching her on the shoulder.

Guests' screams brought staff members rushing into the room.

Carrie slid to her knees and gathered up the fallen books—the attendees' published works Faith had spent so much time arranging for Sunday afternoon's book signing.

Marlene burst into the room. "What's going on here?"

"We had a little accident." Faith motioned toward the fallen bookcase and instantly regretted the movement. She kneaded her shoulder muscle, hoping to make the sharp pain dissipate faster. Then she turned to Pierce, who was straightening his sleeve cuff, thankfully looking none the worse for wear. "Are you okay?"

Pierce gave her a sideways glance that seemed a tad derisive. "I'm fine." Then to her surprise, he told Marlene, "Her quick thinking spared me from injury."

Faith glanced around the room and noticed Tara staring at them. Feeling discomfited by the attention, Faith helped Carrie right the bookcase, and the throb in her shoulder intensified. She knew she should probably go down to the kitchen and put some ice on it before it started to swell.

Marlene made a beeline to Cybil. "Was this one of your planned stunts?" she demanded. "Guest safety is more important than your little games."

"No, I swear it wasn't," Cybil said. To the guests, she suggested, "Perhaps we could start making our way to the dining room now to give the staff some space to straighten things up."

Half the people meandered out. The other half lingered, getting a front-row seat as Marlene unleashed her wrath on Faith.

"You have to be more careful and ensure the bookcases are stable. We can't have this happen again. Understood?"

"Yes, of course." Faith wanted to say she had. She always did. But clearly she hadn't this time.

"It's not her fault," a stylishly dressed man chimed in. He had brown hair and appeared to be in his early forties. "Baltimore tends to rouse bad karma wherever he goes."

A number of guests laughed.

The man smiled at Faith. "By the way, I'm Nolan Shepherd, the only literary agent in attendance. I specialize in acquiring horror writers."

Faith nodded to him. When he turned his attention elsewhere, she pulled Marlene aside and lowered her voice. "What did you mean by stunts? What sort of stunts has Cybil planned?" She hoped they wouldn't endanger the library or its contents.

Marlene waved her hand as if swatting away the notion like a pesky fly. "Cybil wants to create a horror atmosphere with a few spine-tingling surprises."

"What kind of surprises?"

"I don't know. I wasn't privy to the planning." Marlene stalked away.

Faith sighed and joined Carrie in resurrecting the book display.

The remaining guests filed out of the room with Tara bringing up the rear. She exited with a final glance their way.

"Do you know that writer?" Faith asked.

Carrie barely looked up. "No. Maybe she isn't published yet."

"She thought she knew you," Faith said. "She asked me your name."

Carrie let out a nervous chuckle. "So much for the adage that people don't notice the help."

Faith returned her attention to the bookcase and noticed two of the books had been slightly damaged in the fall. She set them aside as a reminder to mend them. After picking up the last book and placing it on the shelf, she stepped back to assess the display.

"Do you need a hand with anything else?" Carrie asked. "I can come back after lunch to stack the chairs."

Faith glanced around. "No, I think that's it. Thank you."

Watson stood at the terrace door, and Faith let him inside. "You missed all the excitement, Rumpy."

The cat didn't dignify the comment with so much as a purr. He obviously wasn't fond of the nickname that emphasized his stubby tail.

"You know it's a term of endearment, right?" she said, trailing him.

Watson pawed at something beneath the bookcase she'd just finished straightening.

"Be careful. I don't want that falling over again." Faith gave it a little shake to test its sturdiness, still mystified at how it had fallen in the first place. Had someone pushed it?

Watson continued pawing at the rug.

Faith stooped next to him. "What did you find?"

The rug beneath one corner of the bookcase had an odd indentation. Faith examined it near the other three corners, but those spots all appeared normal. It looked as if someone had wedged a triangular doorstop under that one corner. But the floor was perfectly level. The bookcase wouldn't have needed it.

She glanced around the floor and under nearby bookcases, but she didn't find any sign of a doorstop. As she picked at the rug fibers to fluff them back up, she thought that the indentation was new.

"Miss Newberry?" a male voice said from behind her.

Faith sprang up and spun around. "May I help you, Mr. Shepherd?"

"Please call me Nolan. I was wondering if you might join my table for lunch."

"Oh, I shouldn't—"

"I already checked with Ms. Russell. She told me it would be all right." Nolan stepped closer and lightly cupped her elbow in his hand. "She said it would give the guests another opportunity to ask you questions."

"Yes, of course." Faith reluctantly accompanied him since Marlene would expect it, even though what she really wanted to do was put an ice pack on her shoulder.

Nolan continued to hold her arm. She'd noticed him schmoozing with a number of women already, so she didn't take his attention too seriously.

"How are you?" he asked as they walked toward the dining room. "I thought I saw that bookcase clip you when it came down."

"Yes, it did." Faith rubbed her shoulder, pleased to realize it was already feeling better. Of course, she'd probably still have a bruise. "But I'm fine."

Nolan shook his head as if he didn't quite believe her but admired her stoicism. "It's not right that you should get injured while trying to spare a scoundrel like Pierce."

"I thought everyone liked Mr. Baltimore. His books are very popular."

"Writers choose to stroke his big ego because they want him as an ally. I, on the other hand, have felt the heat of flying too close to the flame."

"What do you mean?" Faith asked.

Nolan gave her a self-indulgent smile. "I was the agent who discovered him, and I got him his first three contracts. But thanks to a little disagreement on his next proposal, he dropped me and contracted with another agent."

"Just before his meteoric rise in the best-seller lists," Faith finished, knowing Pierce's fourth book was the one that had caused him to break out, as they said in the publishing world.

"Exactly. But I can't complain too much. It boosted sales of his earlier books, and I still get to collect my share of his royalties on those." Nolan motioned for her to precede him into the dining room. "My table is to the left over there."

As he escorted her to a seat, laughter broke out on the other side of the dining room. It was coming from Pierce's table and soon rippled across the room. His fellow diners pointed at the chopsticks standing straight up in his rice.

"What's so funny?" Faith asked.

"It's a death omen," the gray-haired woman sitting beside Faith said. "Pierce wrote a story about it in his new release *Superstition*."

"Do you think Pierce is superstitious?" a woman across the table asked. She reached for the basket of bread and knocked over a saltshaker.

The other authors at the table giggled.

The woman wrung her hands. "Oh no, that's what I get for laughing at his plight."

"Toss some of the spilled salt over your shoulder and nothing bad will happen," another guest instructed.

The woman did as she was told. She was pale, as if she seriously feared bad luck would befall her simply for spilling a little salt.

"Do you ever wonder how these old superstitions began?" Faith asked Nolan. "I'm thinking a mother started the one about spilled salt in an effort to stop her rambunctious children from wasting their precious supply."

"I heard it was because Judas spilled the salt at the Last Supper," Nolan answered. "At least that's how da Vinci painted it." He grinned.

One of the servers set a bowl of butternut squash soup in front of Faith. It was one of her favorite recipes. She dipped in her spoon, then gasped at the sight of something rolling to the surface—an eyeball.

"I think it's plastic, dear," the gray-haired woman beside her said. "I'm Eudora, by the way."

Faith couldn't imagine why this sweet woman was interested in creepy tales.

"I'm afraid we'll have to endure these horror-themed antics throughout the retreat," Eudora continued.

Faith fished the eyeball out of her soup, set it on her bread plate, and tried to ignore it as she ate a spoonful of soup. It was no good. She couldn't do it. Even though she knew the prank was silly, she lost her appetite anyway. For some reason, she still couldn't shake her sense of foreboding.

Faith lingered long enough to not appear rude, then thanked Nolan for his invitation and excused herself.

She hoped Cybil Crypt's practical jokes didn't extend to the beach or the gardens, because she desperately needed a quiet walk.

3

Having her own cottage on the Castleton estate was a perk of the librarian's job Faith definitely appreciated. She could stroll along the beach, enjoy a hike in the woods, or even take one of the horses out for a ride.

Following her afternoon stint in the library, she opted for a leisurely walk on one of the estate's more secluded trails. Unfortunately, even the crunch of fallen leaves beneath her feet made her glance over her shoulder.

And it didn't help that an inordinate number of crows seemed to be gathering in the trees overhead. Surely Cybil wouldn't have brought in a flock of screeching blackbirds in an attempt to recreate a scene from Alfred Hitchcock's *The Birds*.

It wasn't like her to feel so anxious. But from the moment Cybil's volunteers started decorating the manor for the retreat, Faith had felt as if she were being dragged into a theater to watch a horror movie marathon against her will. Every direction she turned, she expected a bat or a spider to jump out at her.

Something touched her shoulder.

Yelping, she lurched sideways and swatted wildly. It was a low-lying branch. Okay, she was definitely way too keyed up. Those horror stories she'd had to skim the past few days to prepare for this morning's lecture hadn't helped either.

Faith shook away the images that sprang to mind and started humming "My Favorite Things" from *The Sound of Music*. After singing under her breath about raindrops on roses and whiskers on kittens more times than she wanted to admit, she moved on to her favorite worship songs.

By the time she finished the loop, she felt totally relaxed. Still, she gave the manor a wide berth to avoid seeing any gruesome displays being set up for the evening's soiree and headed to the gardener's cottage she called home.

As she passed by the kennels, Pierce emerged with an energetic border collie on a leash. Someone who took his dog for a walk couldn't be as arrogant as Nolan had made him out to be. Could he?

Midge and her new sidekick walked out of the horse stalls and waved.

"Do you have time to join me for a cup of tea?" Faith called out.

"Sorry. I have to go. See you tomorrow." Bill tapped the brim of his baseball cap, then walked toward the parking lot.

Midge ran her fingers through her blonde hair, removing bits of hay. "I'm afraid I can't. Sarah just called. A water pipe burst." Sarah Goodwin was the manager at Midge's pet bakery and her most trusted employee.

"Oh no. I hope she got the water shut off before it did any damage."

Midge climbed inside her SUV. "Yeah, me too. I'll see you later."

Faith followed the estate's main driveway the rest of the way to her cottage and was about to turn onto her short driveway when Wolfe pulled up in his dark blue BMW and rolled down his window.

She smiled. "It's good to see you back," she said, then wondered if the comment sounded too familiar. The man was her boss, even if Brooke liked to read more into his occasional invitations for Faith to join him at some of the manor's special events. After all, they were always related to work.

"It's good to be back," Wolfe said. "Are you busy tonight?"

She ignored the silly uptick in her pulse. "No. Why?"

"A bookdealer is stopping by with a selection of rare editions he hopes he can interest me in."

"Oh, nice. Are you thinking of adding them to the library's collection?"

"That's right." Wolfe reached for a piece of paper on the seat beside him and held it up. "I was hoping you could go over the descriptions with me before he comes and help me assess which ones we might want."

"Sure. I'd be happy to help." Faith loved his enthusiasm for growing the library's collection. Budget restraints at her last library had made gaining approval for new acquisitions a constant challenge. She closed the distance between them and examined the list he passed to her.

"Would you mind staying to check out the books too?" he asked, sounding apologetic for the seeming imposition. "So you can ensure they're worth what he's asking."

"Absolutely." She handed the list back to him. "Some of these books would make fabulous additions to the library."

"I'm glad to hear it. How about you come up to the manor in about an hour? I'll ask the staff to bring two dinners to my apartment so we can eat as we work."

"That sounds lovely."

"Great. See you then." Wolfe smiled and drove off.

An odd fluttering of foliage jolted Faith's attention from Wolfe's disappearing car. As she peered at the shrubs circling the manor, her heart mimicked their odd flutter. Cautiously, she wandered over to investigate.

A giant lion-shaped topiary swooped above the row of hedges.

Faith jumped back.

Cybil poked her head around the hedge. "Sorry. I didn't mean to scare you." She grinned as she stepped into view, looking anything but scary in a bright lime-green dress and heels. "Not yet anyway."

Against her instincts, Faith peeked around the end of the hedge to see what Cybil had been up to. Tara was prying her head from the lion's jaws. Faith gulped.

"It's part of a gag," Cybil explained. "Like the lion topiary that comes to life in Stephen King's *The Shining*, remember?"

Faith nodded, even though she had no idea. She'd never read the book or dared watch the movie it had inspired.

Tara walked up to them. "Faith could help us," she suggested.

Faith raised her hands and backed away. "Oh no, I don't like to be frightened."

"Then you'd be perfect," Tara said.

"Yes," Cybil agreed. "All we need you to do is run into the manor and act terrified over the topiary that's attacking someone so the others will come out and see for themselves."

"I really can't. I have to rush home now so I can make a meeting at the manor with the owner about possible new library acquisitions in an hour . . ." Knowing she was babbling, Faith let her voice trail off.

"That will work out great," Cybil said. "You can do it as you're going into the manor for your meeting."

Faith's heart thumped. "I don't know. The idea of lying to scare—"

"You wouldn't be lying," Cybil interrupted. "The topiary is animated. I had it specially made for our retreat." Grinning, she tapped a button on the remote control she held. "See? So you *will* witness it attack Tara. Besides, it's acting and all in good fun."

"Okay, I guess I can do that." Faith sighed, miffed at herself for caving in to their request. She wasn't a stick-in-the-mud, but she knew she would feel ridiculous trying to act frightened in front of the guests.

As she trudged home, a familiar black-and-white figure appeared next to her on the path.

She smiled. "Where have you been, Watson?"

The cat rubbed against her ankles and purred.

When the pair arrived at the cottage, Watson dashed into the kitchen and meowed, reminding her of her neglect.

"Sorry." She followed him into the kitchen and filled his dishes. "I'm afraid I'll be out tonight. Are you going to be a good boy while I'm gone?"

He didn't answer, and Faith had no illusions of him keeping his word if he had. Watson always seemed to get into mischief.

Leaving Watson to eat his dinner, Faith hurried to get ready.

When she arrived at the front door in clean clothes with freshly done hair and a touch of makeup—it was a meeting with her boss, after all—Watson was already waiting there. She grabbed her coat and opened the door.

Watson immediately darted out.

"This means you'll be out until I get back," she called after him.

The cat scampered off as if he didn't care.

Faith locked the door and paused, taking a deep breath. She drank in the brilliant reds and oranges streaking the sky and tried to fortify herself with happy non-horror thoughts. She trekked to the manor via a route that took her past the manor's collection of topiaries—leafy sculptures of famous authors and people reading books. They were far more sedate than Cybil's lion.

As if thinking about Cybil's custom-made topiary brought it to life, the lion lunged above the row of hedges.

Since Faith didn't see Tara or hear her screaming, she was about to peek around the hedge when Cybil caught her attention from the terrace.

Cybil waved her forward, miming acting frightened.

Feeling foolish, Faith rushed into the manor, where the retreat guests were talking and milling around. She feigned fright and babbled nonsense about a topiary attacking someone. "It's in the topiary garden. One of the sculptures—" Faith broke off and covered her face with her hands as if what she'd seen was too horrible.

The guests gaped at her for a moment, then surged toward the garden en masse.

Wolfe chuckled as he joined Faith. "Well done. I had no idea you were such a talented actress."

Faith's cheeks heated.

Before she could explain how she'd gotten involved in the gag, screaming erupted from the topiary garden, followed by orders to call 911.

"Oh no," Faith said. "We'd better tell them it's a prank before someone actually calls. The police and paramedics won't appreciate being summoned under false pretenses."

Marlene stepped up to them. "It's okay. Ms. Crypt assured me that she made arrangements with the police chief to use the call as a drill."

"Seriously?" Faith glanced back at the scene unfolding in the distance and shook her head. "I'm surprised Cybil picked a sensible reporter like Tara to be her victim. Horror flicks typically kill off foolish teenagers first, don't they?"

Wolfe chuckled again.

At the sound of approaching sirens, Wolfe said, "Let's leave the writers to their games and get started on reviewing that list."

Gladly. Faith followed him up to his luxurious third-floor apartment, where a delicious-smelling dinner was already waiting for them.

Wolfe ushered her over to the table for two by one of the many windows overlooking the grounds, then held out a chair for her.

Faith sat down and turned her attention to the view outside. She could see the emergency vehicles' flashing lights winding through town from here. "I hope Marlene is right about Cybil making prior arrangements with them."

"Marlene's nothing if not efficient. I'd be surprised if she hasn't double- and triple-checked it herself." Wolfe removed the warming covers from their plates and sat opposite her. "I hope you like Alaskan salmon."

Faith regarded the meal. The salmon was the perfect color, with a creamy sauce drizzled artfully over it. Wild rice and steamed broccoli with melted cheese rounded out the plate. "I love it. Thank you."

"My pleasure. Let's eat before it gets cold."

"May I read over that list while we eat?" she asked.

"Oh, you don't need to do that," he protested. "It's bad enough I stole you away from your quiet evening at home."

"Bribed me with the offer of delicious food and potentially acquiring new books, you mean," she corrected him. "Really, I insist. I enjoy reading while I eat anyway."

Wolfe laughed. "Who am I to refuse an employee so passionate in the performance of her duties?" He handed her the paper he'd shown her earlier. "Which novels would be your top picks from this list?"

"Definitely the first edition of *To Kill a Mockingbird*. I think I was about thirteen when I first read it, and I can still remember how it gripped me. *The Trumpet of the Swan* by E. B. White is another favorite of mine. My mom read it to my sister and me at night in our tent one summer when we went camping."

"Yes, it occurred to me that we have very few children's novels in our collection, besides Mark Twain's."

Was that a hint of longing in his voice? She wondered if Wolfe's mother had ever read books to him and his brothers. Faith had such fond memories of her parents reading to her and her sister. She hated to imagine what might have become of the Jaxon family's library—to say nothing of her job—if Wolfe didn't share the same love of books.

Outside, the commotion rose to such a fever pitch that they could hear it through the third-story windows.

Faith peered out. "It's a good thing you live on a large estate or your neighbors might start complaining."

Wolfe frowned down at the gardens, then pulled his phone from his pocket. "I'll ask Marlene to urge them to dial it back a few degrees."

Marlene's panicked voice exploded from his phone. "I was just about to call you. You need to get down here now."

"What's wrong?" Wolfe asked, then glanced at the phone. "She hung up on me. We'd better go see what's happening."

They swiftly boarded the elevator. It seemed to move in slow motion, or maybe it was the contrast to Faith's racing heart. The instant the doors opened, they rushed toward the lobby.

Marlene hurried in from the yard at the same time, her face ashen.

"What's going on?" Wolfe demanded.

"She's dead. For real."

4

Faith's heart lurched at Marlene's words.

"Slow down," Wolfe told Marlene. "Who's dead?"

"Tara. The paramedics and police were doing their thing, knowing it was all supposed to be a drill." Marlene pressed her fingertips to her lips, clearly fighting to control her emotions. "But the paramedics realized right away that something was actually wrong. She had no pulse and wasn't breathing. She's dead!"

"Stay here," Wolfe said to both of them, and he strode outside.

Marlene wrung her hands. "I can't believe this is happening. It's as if we're cursed."

"Calm down," Faith said. "You've been listening to too many of their superstitious ramblings. We're not cursed." But even as she said it, her thoughts ridiculously skittered to the hole in the baker's bread.

"You met Tara. She was young and healthy," Marlene insisted. "How could her heart just stop?"

"There was no sign of trauma?"

"That's what the paramedics said. But I'm sure that won't stop the police from crawling all over the place for the next few days," Marlene added derisively, sounding like her old self again.

"They're only doing their job. And I'm sure the autopsy will show that something actually happened to her." Faith peeked out the window beside the door just as Wolfe and Police Chief Andy Garris climbed the terrace steps, exhaustion on their faces.

Wolfe opened the door for the chief, then said to Faith, "I told the chief that you might have been the last person to see Miss Blue alive besides Ms. Crypt, but she's a little too hysterical at the moment to be of any help."

"I need to ask you some questions," Chief Garris said.

Faith respected the chief and was grateful for his calming presence, but her heart still thudded double time. "Yes, of course."

"I'd better see to Ms. Crypt and the other guests," Marlene said. She slipped outside before anyone could protest.

"I'm going to call the bookdealer," Wolfe said to Faith, "and reschedule our meeting for another night."

Faith nodded.

The chief prodded Faith toward a group of chairs in the corner of the lobby. She complied, too stunned to do otherwise. They sat down across from each other.

Chief Garris took out a notepad and a pen. "How well did you know the victim?"

"Not well. I met her yesterday. She arrived with her cat—oh, her cat. We need to—"

"Miss Newberry, calm down. The cat can wait. We'll ensure he's taken care of."

"It's a she."

"What can you tell me about Miss Blue?" he asked, his voice rising with annoyance.

Faith ducked her head. She'd never heard Chief Garris be so short with anyone, and she didn't like being responsible for it. But she supposed it was understandable that he was more than a little tense. He had been under the impression that his men were responding to the 911 call as a training exercise, but they had been confronted with an actual victim instead. "All I know is that she's a reporter and an aspiring novelist."

"A reporter, huh? Do you know of anyone who might have wanted to hurt her?"

Faith stared at the chief. "You think she was killed?"

"We won't know until we get the autopsy results. In the meantime, we need to cover all our bases. When did you last see Miss Blue?"

"About four thirty."

Garris jotted down notes. "Did she seem distraught in any way?"

"No. She and Cybil were setting up a practical joke with the animated topiary and asked if I'd play along about an hour later to draw the guests outside."

"Cybil Crypt?"

"Yes."

"Did you see anyone else in the area?"

"No."

"And an hour later, what did you see?"

"I saw the topiary moving, and I was about to look around the hedge to see if Tara was ready for me to summon the guests when Cybil waved me into action from the terrace."

"She was the only other person you saw in the vicinity?"

Faith cringed at how that sounded. "Yes. But I can't imagine any reason why Cybil would want Tara dead."

"Like I said before, at this point we're merely gathering information and evidence."

Officer Bryan Laddy burst into the lobby. "Chief, a vial and seven needles were in the victim's jacket pocket." He rushed over to them and handed the chief a plastic bag.

"Tara's cat is diabetic," Faith said. "Those needles and the vial are for the cat. Midge gave them to Tara because she forgot to bring Midnight's insulin from home." She shot a worried glance up the main staircase, as if she might see through the floor to the poor motherless cat. "I should call Midge to come and see to the cat. I don't know when Midnight is supposed to get her next dose of insulin."

"Okay, call her," the chief said, then inspected the contents of the bag.

Before Faith walked away to make the call, she noticed that the vial looked nearly full.

Midge picked up on the first ring, and Faith explained the situation.

"I'm in the middle of dealing with a birthing mare at the moment, but don't worry. Midnight will be okay. She only gets a dose of insulin twice a day with meals. Just don't feed her, and I'll check in on her as soon as I can. Before breakfast at the latest. Okay?"

"Yes, as long as you're sure she'll be all right."

"Midnight will be fine. Have them bed her down at the kennels tonight. I'll let the staff know about her special needs."

"Will do. Thanks." Faith disconnected the call.

The instant Faith rejoined the chief, he flipped a page on his notepad and started in with his questions again. "What was Miss Blue wearing when you saw her last?"

Faith frowned. "I'm not sure. I didn't pay much attention."

Chief Garris lowered his voice as returning guests encroached on their quiet corner. "Do you know if she has a boyfriend?"

"No, I have no idea. I had just met her yesterday."

"She used to date Nolan Shepherd," Eudora, the lady Faith had sat beside at lunch, piped up.

"He's a literary agent," Faith added by way of explanation. "And he's here this weekend." She pointed him out to the chief.

Garris closed his notepad. "Okay, that's all for now. But I might have more questions for you later."

"May I fetch Tara's cat from her guest room? Midge asked that she be taken to the kennels."

"Yes, go ahead."

Faith approached the front desk. She borrowed the master key and found out that Tara had been staying in the Emily Dickinson Suite, then went up to the second floor.

Watson was crouched outside the door to Tara's room, shoving his paw underneath and pulling it back, then tapping the black paw that peeked out beneath the door.

Faith's heart cracked at the sweet sight. "Did you know she'd be sad?" she asked Watson. "Is that what brought you up here?"

When Faith opened the door, Midnight cowered and trembled. "It's okay, sweetie," Faith soothed. "I'm Watson's mistress. You remember me."

At Watson's meow, Midnight stopped trembling and crept a few inches closer.

"Good girl. We need to take you down to the kennels for the night, so Midge can check in on you." Faith gathered Midnight into her arms, grateful the cat didn't feel the need to project her claws.

Watson trotted along beside them down the stairs.

In the lobby, Cybil was petitioning Marlene for permission to carry on with her plans for the rest of the retreat.

Marlene turned to the chief. "What do you think?"

Faith held her breath. A veto from Garris could mean this horrible retreat might be over almost before it started.

The chief shrugged. "I don't see why not. At this point, we have no reason to suspect foul play, and it would better ensure the guests remain here if we need to question them further."

Marlene passed the green light on to Cybil.

Faith strode through the lobby without talking to anyone, wondering where Wolfe had gone.

The ambulance pulled away as Faith stepped outside. Thankful she didn't have to deal with the cat seeing her mistress's body, Faith hugged the feline a little closer.

She walked by two guests still milling around the terrace.

"She's not really dead," one of them announced. "This is a retreat for horror writers. You know they want to spook us. But they also know we'll be skeptical of everything we hear. So what better way to make us think a murder happened? Mark my words. It's all a ruse."

Could that be true? Would the chief play along like this? Faith shook her head, remembering how upset Tara had been over forgetting Midnight's insulin. Tara wouldn't have risked leaving her cat unattended just to play out a silly caper. Would she?

Suddenly Midge's story about the birthing mare sounded a little fishy too. Why hadn't she called Bill to come back and check on Midnight?

The next morning Watson scratched at the front door, seeming especially anxious to get out.

"Are you planning to visit your new girlfriend?" Faith smiled as she opened the door for him.

He took off toward the kennels, confirming her suspicions.

Cybil had a yacht tour planned for the guests that morning, so Marlene had told Faith not to open the library until after lunch. In the meantime, she planned to have a quiet morning and maybe run to town for supplies to repair the books that had been damaged when the bookcase had fallen.

She sat down with her tea and devotional book, hoping for a little solace. Halfway through the night, she'd realized she was in denial that Tara was really dead, just like the guests she'd overheard. After all, she hadn't seen the body. But the more she thought about it, the more certain she was that the chief and Wolfe wouldn't lie about something like that, especially to her since she was an employee of the manor.

The phone rang, making her jump.

"I'm at the kennels with Midnight and Watson," Midge said. "He's doing a good job of cheering her up, by the way. But the staff said she was anxious all night, so I was wondering if you could bring some clothing of Tara's for her to sleep with. Having the scent of her mistress should give Midnight some measure of comfort."

"Absolutely. I'll get to the manor now." Faith disconnected, then hurried to Castleton.

As Faith stepped inside, she noticed the lobby was eerily quiet. Everyone must have already headed down to the dock. Faith went to the front desk for the master key, but it wasn't there. One of the other staff members had probably borrowed it. She headed toward the main staircase, hoping she'd find a housekeeper upstairs who could let her into Tara's room.

Carrie stood in front of a bulletin board set on an easel beside the foot of the stairs, her eyes wide and a hand over her heart.

Faith joined her. "What's wrong?" The bulletin board displayed snapshots of guests from the previous couple of days.

Carrie pointed to one of the photographs. "Tara is in the middle of three people."

"So?"

"The Japanese believe that if you take a picture of three people, the one in the middle will die soon."

Faith shivered, even though she didn't share Carrie's belief in such superstitions.

"Pierce Baltimore wrote a story about it in his newest book," Carrie went on. "It's creepy. Don't you think?"

Faith squinted at the photo, wondering if Cybil deliberately took it to *make* the superstition "come true" via Tara's fake death. If so, certainly Cybil would have had the decency to take down the picture after what happened.

Bothered by how visibly shaken Carrie was, Faith scanned the remaining photos, searching for some words of comfort or wisdom or something to offer her. She gestured to a photo with Pierce in the middle of a group of three guests. "Do you think Pierce would have posed for this picture if he believed in the superstition? It would mean he'd die soon too."

Carrie gasped.

Faith scolded herself for not providing the most sensible counterargument. She decided that distraction would be better. "I need to get into Tara's room to take a piece of her clothing to the kennels to comfort her cat. Would you mind letting me in?"

"Sure. I was on my way to clean guest rooms before I got sidetracked by the pictures." Carrie hustled up the stairs. "I guess I should be glad it was you who caught me and not Ms. Russell. She doesn't seem like the understanding type. And she's in a really bad mood today."

"I suspect last night's events have us all a little on edge," Faith said.

At the top of the stairs, Carrie paused with her keys in hand. "Do you remember which suite Tara was in?"

"Emily Dickinson," Faith replied.

"Oh yes, now I remember." Carrie turned left.

"No, it's this way," Faith said, turning right and leading the way. But the door to the suite wasn't latched. "Is someone else cleaning rooms up here?"

"I don't think so." Carrie pushed the door all the way open.

Inside, Pierce stood at the desk, searching through Tara's papers.

"Looking for another story?" Carrie said caustically. Then she quickly dropped her gaze and backed out of the doorway.

"Mr. Baltimore, may I ask what you're doing in here?" Faith said as she entered the room.

"The door was unlocked," Pierce answered, scarcely sparing her a glance.

"That doesn't give you the right to come in and go through Tara's belongings," Faith said.

Pierce stopped his rummaging and raised his hands. "Hey, I'm not stealing anything. I offered to pay tribute to Tara tomorrow morning by reading one of her stories."

Carrie's snort carried from the hallway.

Faith wasn't sure she believed him either. It didn't help matters that she might be to blame. Maybe she'd forgotten to lock the door when she retrieved Midnight from Tara's room.

"Carrie, what are you doing standing around?" Marlene's sharp voice ricocheted off the walls.

Faith glanced out the door and saw Carrie hurrying off to her cleaning cart.

Marlene entered the suite and frowned. "What is going on here?"
Pierce repeated his story.

Marlene's expression softened. "It sounds like a nice idea. But may I suggest we wait until Tara's mother arrives to collect her daughter's things? Then we can ask her for permission, and she might have a recommendation on which work to share."

Pierce made a face, clearly finding her proposal distasteful, but he didn't argue.

Marlene ushered him from the room with her practiced diplomacy.

Faith straightened Tara's papers. In one folder, there was an eclectic collection of articles by other reporters, perhaps as inspiration for her stories or for articles of her own. They were on everything from a runaway boy's death in a boat fire to a story on the latest fashion trends.

Marlene poked her head into the room again. "What are you still doing here?"

"Midge asked me to take an article of clothing to the kennels to help comfort Tara's cat," Faith explained.

"All right, get a move on so I can lock this room."

Faith grabbed a T-shirt flung over the bed and dashed out of the room. She flew down the stairs and almost knocked Bill over in her headlong rush out the main door. "I'm so sorry."

"It's all right." Bill pointed to the T-shirt in her hand. "Is that for Midnight?"

"Yes, I was just on my way to the kennels with it."

"I can take it. Midge had to go to the pet bakery to meet a plumber."

"Thanks, but I don't mind delivering it. I should probably make sure Watson isn't getting into any trouble down there anyway."

"The tuxedo cat?"

"Oh no. What did he do this time?"

Bill chuckled. "Nothing that I know of. But Cybil stopped by to ask if we had a barn cat who'd want to go on a boat ride, and when she said the word *fish*, Watson sort of volunteered."

Faith shook her head. "What was she thinking? Cats hate water."

"I guess she's about to find that out."

The cat batted at the giant bauble dangling from the woman's neck. He didn't normally let anyone other than his human carry him anywhere, but this person smelled almost as good as his human's friend who owned the shop where she bought his tunaroons.

The human pulled another treat from her pocket and held it out to him.

He took it from her fingers, being careful not to nip them, and nibbled slowly to savor the taste.

Just as he was about to paw at her hand to ask for another, the sound of her steps changed. He shot a startled glance at the dock beneath her feet, or rather the water below it, and reared back in her arms.

"It's okay, kitty," she said, squeezing his middle. "You'll like the boat. There are lots of people aboard who will make a fuss over you. Besides, a cat on a boat is considered good luck. I'm not sure why."

The cat huffed. He could smell a fish a mile away. Of course he was good luck on a boat.

The aroma of raw fish tickled his nostrils, and he sat up taller in her arms, searching for the source. He spotted a cooler being loaded onto the boat in front of them and decided maybe being close to the water wouldn't be so bad. After all, it wasn't as if his human was here to give him a bath.

A man in a baseball cap cut in front of them and pointed a camera at them. "Smile."

The cat intentionally averted his gaze.

"Good morning, Watson," said a familiar, rumbly voice. The nice human from the manor stood on the boat. "Is your mistress joining us too?"

The woman holding the cat said, "Isn't he a barn cat? I found him at the kennels."

The man chuckled. "No, he belongs to Faith Newberry, our librarian."

He ruffled the cat's fur as the woman holding him boarded the boat. "Or should I say she belongs to you?"

The cat purred. He liked this human.

A person toted the fish cooler past them, and the cat jumped from the woman's arms and followed. When the man set the cooler down, the cat leaped onto the seat beside it.

The boat soon bobbed away from shore. The cat dug his claws into the seat and scowled at the human who'd brought him aboard.

The man standing beside her at the boat's railing began whistling.

"Now you've gone and done it," another human griped.

"Done what?" the whistler retorted.

"You're not supposed to whistle on deck. It means a storm is coming. Everyone knows that."

The cat looked at the sky and then around the boat for a place to shelter from the rain if the human turned out to be right.

After some time went by with no rain falling, the cat pawed at the corner of the cooler, hoping for another snack.

The human who'd carried the cooler aboard chuckled, then flipped open the lid and tossed the cat a fish head. "Is this what you're after?"

The cat pounced on the treat. Halfway through, he realized the human had started throwing the others overboard. So the cat jumped into the cooler and splayed his paws over as many as he could.

"Sorry, fella, but these are shark bait." The man scooped the cat out of the cooler and plopped him back onto the seat cushion, but at least he gave him another fish head as a consolation prize.

The other humans gawked over the side of the boat, gasping and pointing.

The cat padded over to investigate. He wanted to yowl at the sight of all the fish heads that had been wasted. But the humans were more enthralled by the machine with the big fin churning around the boat. It mimicked a big fish, except that it completely ignored the fish heads and sounded like his human's vacuum cleaner.

The cat returned to his fish. After he finished, he proceeded to clean his fur. A gray-haired woman gaped at him in horror.

The cat glanced around to see what was wrong. He noticed nothing amiss, so he returned to his grooming.

"He's licking his fur backward," the woman squeaked. "That means a bad storm is coming."

Faith drove into Lighthouse Bay to pay her aunt Eileen a visit at the Candle House Library and to see if she had some spare supplies so Faith could mend the two books that had been slightly damaged when the bookcase fell.

When she was a couple of blocks away from her destination, she noticed a well-dressed man wandering the street as if lost. She was surprised to see that it was Nolan.

Faith parked and caught up to him. "Is everything okay? I thought you'd be on the yacht with the others."

Nolan stared at her for a full three seconds before he seemed to register who she was. "I didn't feel right about going because of Tara's death and not knowing the cause. I tried to call Tara's mother to offer my condolences and whatever help I can, but there was no answer. So I came to town to find a florist to send flowers."

"That's nice of you," Faith said. "There's a florist down the street. I'm heading that way to visit my aunt at the library. I can show you."

His shoulders visibly relaxed. "Thank you. I appreciate it." He fell into step beside her. "I've been feeling a little out of sorts since Tara's death. We actually dated for a while."

"I'm sorry for your loss," Faith said. She'd already heard about their relationship, but she didn't want to tell Nolan that people had been talking about him.

"I was the only one there last night who knew her as more than a passing acquaintance," he remarked.

Faith realized that fact also made him a significant person of interest if the death turned out to be murder. She imagined the police had a lot of questions for him either way.

"We were still friends," Nolan continued. "It wasn't as if we had a messy breakup or anything. We went out for a few months and enjoyed spending time together, but neither of us really felt that spark. You know what I mean?"

Faith nodded. "Did she ever mention having a heart condition?"

"Who told you that?"

"No one. I was just wondering if—"

"Tara was in excellent health," he interrupted. "She ran a marathon last year."

"So you don't think she died of natural causes?" Faith asked.

"Let's just say I find it as hard to believe as the idea that anyone would want to hurt her." Nolan tilted his head and slowed his pace, studying Faith. "I heard you have a reputation for solving mysteries."

"Where did you hear that?"

Nolan stuffed his hands into his pockets. "One of the servers at breakfast said if there was foul play involved, we could count on you to sniff it out."

Faith didn't know how to respond. It was true that she'd helped the police in the past, but she didn't go around seeking out crimes to solve. "I'm sure the coroner's autopsy will clear up any mystery."

"When someone as sweet as Tara dies in the prime of her life, no answer will ever be satisfactory." His voice cracked, indicating he cared more deeply for her than his earlier comment had suggested.

What if the decision to break up hadn't been mutual? Some people were so possessive of the one they supposedly loved that if they couldn't have them, they'd sooner see them dead than with someone else. Faith shivered at the thought.

"Are you cold?" Nolan asked.

"I'm just not used to the cooler weather yet." Faith zipped the light windbreaker she wore.

They reached the flower shop, and Faith pointed at the building. "This is the place you want."

"Thanks. I guess I'll see you later."

"I'll have the library open this afternoon."

The first hint of a lighter mood flitted in his eyes. "No more toppling bookcases?"

Heat streaked up Faith's neck. "No, I assure you that you'll be perfectly safe."

Nolan grinned. "It wouldn't have been so bad to see a book or two bounce off Baltimore's swollen head." He winked and then entered the shop.

Faith continued down the street. Delicious aromas of fresh-baked bread and cinnamon rolls wafted from the door of Snickerdoodles Bakery & Tea Shop, and Faith couldn't resist the temptation to stop in.

Owner Jane McGee was busy loading cupcakes into a box for a customer, but she waved to Faith. "Good morning. I'll be with you in a moment."

Faith took the opportunity to stroll along the glass display cases, trying to decide which of the mouthwatering goodies to choose.

"How are you doing?" Jane asked Faith after the previous customer exited. "I heard you had a tragedy at the manor last night."

"Yes, it was so sad."

Jane nodded. "I'm not the superstitious type, but it would have been even creepier if it had happened today."

"Why? What's today?"

"Friday the thirteenth."

"Oh, right. I imagine they'll make a big to-do about the date at the retreat."

Jane offered her an empathetic look. "Just think, a few more days and it'll all be a distant memory."

Not for Tara's family and friends, Faith thought.

"So what can I get you today?"

"I'm on my way to see Eileen. She loves apple and cinnamon, so I'm thinking we should try that streusel muffin there. I'll take two."

"Good choice. They're still warm." Jane put them in a bag and rang up the bill. She smiled as she handed Faith the bag and her change.

After saying goodbye, Faith slipped into the Candle House Library next door.

Aunt Eileen bustled out from her favorite section—the mysteries. "Is that apple and cinnamon I smell?"

"Yes, I was hoping we could share them over a cup of tea." Faith handed her the bag of muffins.

"That sounds wonderful. Are you sure you don't have an ulterior motive?" her aunt teased.

Faith tried to suppress a smile. "Now that you mention it, I was wondering if you have any spare supplies I can use to repair a couple of damaged books."

Eileen laughed. "Of course." She glanced toward her part-time employee Gail. "I'll be in my office if you need me." Eileen was the head librarian in the privately funded library and could basically choose her break times at will.

When they entered Eileen's office, Faith wandered over to the window. She was a little surprised to see Nolan standing on the corner, gazing at the library.

Aunt Eileen motioned Faith to the round table in the corner. "Have a seat while I put on the kettle."

Faith sat down and glanced at the photocopies spread out on the table. Upon closer inspection, she realized they were all magazine articles written by Tara. "Why do I get the feeling you were expecting me?"

Eileen joined her with the muffins on two small plates, her eyes twinkling. "You know I can't resist a good mystery. But Chief Garris asked me to gather these articles for him. He thought they might offer a clue to who had motive to kill the poor dear."

"He said that? They've decided she was murdered?"

"To be honest"—Eileen lowered her voice even though they were alone in the room—"I don't believe the police know what to think. I heard the autopsy offered no clue as to what caused her death, and I think they've widened the net on what drugs they're testing her for. In the meantime, I suspect Garris is just fishing for plausible suspects in case they find something."

Faith scanned the titles of the articles. "Tara certainly had a diverse portfolio. She wrote about everything from the resurging popularity of the horror novel to suspected mafia-tied bribes in awarding city contracts."

Eileen scooped up the latter story. "I highlighted a couple of names in this one. I figured anything tied to organized crime could wind up with someone wearing cement shoes."

Faith took a bite of her muffin as she skimmed the piece. "But I suspect these government officials whose names you highlighted are more worried about what the mob might do to them than Tara's article."

"I wouldn't be so sure. There are rumblings that the fallout from this article could cost the implicated official his seat in the next election."

Faith studied the man's picture that was included with the story. "I haven't seen him hanging around Castleton."

"He wouldn't though, would he? If the mob has him in their pocket, they'd want to ensure he keeps his seat. So they'd send one of their guys to take care of Tara."

Faith frowned. "Why bother? The damage has already been done. It isn't as if killing Tara would help undo it. If anything, it would prove she was right, wouldn't it?"

"Ah, that's where you'd be wrong." Eileen tapped the notation at the bottom of the story. "This was part one of three. I imagine the next installment was probably soon to be released."

Faith snatched up the article. "Good catch. Did you show this to the chief?"

Eileen grinned. "I sure did."

The kettle whistled, and Eileen took it off the heat.

Faith perused the remaining stories. "I think Pierce Baltimore might know something," she said after reading an article Tara had written about his writing process and latest release.

"Why's that?"

"Tara wrote a glowing story about him. Any author should be grateful for the free publicity, right?"

"Absolutely."

"Yet the morning Tara died, I saw the two of them in a heated argument."

Eileen brought over the teapot and two teacups. After pouring a cup for each of them, she set the teapot in the center of the table. "The timing does make that sound suspicious."

"That and the fact I saw Pierce out walking his dog not long before I ran into Tara and Cybil in the topiary garden. He was bound to have crossed paths with them too when he returned to the manor. Not to mention I found him in Tara's room, searching her papers this morning."

"Why was he going through her papers?"

"He claimed he was trying to find a story to read as a tribute to her."

Eileen settled into a chair and nibbled on her muffin. "Yes, that definitely sounds suspicious. Who is Cybil?"

Faith told her and then explained the prank Cybil and Tara had been getting ready to play on the guests.

"It sounds like we should take a closer look at Cybil too."

"I don't know. I doubt Tara would have cooperated with Cybil's plans if the woman had something against her. But Cybil would be my first suspect if Pierce had been the one who died. She holds a giant grudge against him and doesn't even try to hide it."

Eileen took a sip of tea. "Is there anyone else suspicious I should know about?"

"There's Nolan Shepherd, a literary agent who dated Tara for a while." Faith wandered over to the window again to see if he was still standing on the corner. He was now on the other corner, chatting with a stocky, dark-haired man. She pointed him out to her aunt.

"Who's he talking to?"

"No clue. I don't recognize him from the retreat."

"He seems like the mob type," Eileen said. "It looks as if his nose has been broken more than once. And why does Nolan keep staring at my library?"

"He knows I came in here." *And thanks to a talkative kitchen helper, he knows I have a penchant for solving mysteries.*

"So he could be waiting for you to come back out." Eileen pulled Faith away from the window.

"I'm not sure what to think about Nolan. He seems very charming and thoughtful."

"Yes, but many clever criminals fool investigators with their charm," Eileen said bluntly.

6

Faith added a log to the fireplace in the Castleton library. Not only did its warmth take the chill out of the room, but it added a glowing ambience that could almost make her forget they were supposed to be celebrating the horror genre this weekend.

Wolfe strode into the library with Watson nestled in his sweater-clad arms. "I thought we'd find you here."

"Uh-oh. What did he do?"

Wolfe laughed, the deep sound chasing away Faith's concerns.

"He was the perfect mascot." Wolfe affectionately scratched Watson's neck. "He successfully roused enough superstitions to give just about everyone in the boat a few butterflies in the stomach."

"You did?" Faith gaped at Watson.

The cat gave her a smug look that seemed to say, "There was nothing to it."

"Cybil was stunned at how well her plan worked. She thinks Watson should be in show business. I think that if he keeps this up, we'll have to start paying him too."

Faith laughed. "You hear that, Watson? She thinks you could be a star." To Wolfe, she added, "Of course, I'd never be able to live with him. His head wouldn't fit through the door."

Wolfe chuckled. "Another Chester."

Faith's eyes widened. "I was thinking that very thing. You know those books?" Mélanie Watt's *Chester* books, featuring a cat that takes over the author's stories, were picture books.

"I bought them for my nieces and nephew one Christmas. I must have read them to Richard's three kids a hundred times by the end of our visit." Wolfe regarded Watson. "I could see you as Chester."

The cat huffed and jumped from Wolfe's arms. He circled the chairs around the fireplace, finally curling up in the middle one.

"So how on earth did Watson stir up these superstitions?" Faith asked. "The only one I know about cats is that you don't want a black one to cross your path. But he isn't even all black."

"I didn't know there were others either. But the guests are certainly aware of them." Wolfe recounted the events of the morning. "The sight of a massive white shark circling the boat didn't worry the group half as much as a little cat licking his fur the wrong way."

"What? You saw a shark?"

His blue eyes twinkled. "It was a prop. Cybil had hoped to be able to attract some real ones by baiting the water, but I told her the ocean temperatures were too cold this far up the coast."

Faith couldn't help but smile. The idea of trying to frighten a hard-core group of horror writers with a fake shark was too funny. Even she might have enjoyed that. "And what does Watson licking his fur backward mean?"

Carrie, who'd slipped into the room with a fresh supply of firewood while they were talking, piped up, "That means there's going to be a storm. A bad one."

Wolfe nodded. "That's why everyone insisted we cut the yacht tour short."

Faith glanced out the window and frowned. "There's scarcely a cloud in the sky." She couldn't understand why people believed all these ridiculous tales.

"I know." Wolfe sounded bewildered too. "But I was afraid I'd have a mutiny on my hands if I didn't give the captain the order to bring us back."

"You were smart to heed the warning," Carrie said solemnly. Then she walked outside through the terrace door.

Faith shot Wolfe a puzzled look. "If she's so convinced a storm is coming, then why did she go outside?"

"Maybe to batten down the hatches." Wolfe grinned. "By the way, I want to try to reschedule with the bookdealer for sometime this weekend. Will you be available to join us?"

"Yes, I can come in whenever you need me."

"Great. I'll let you know," he said, then glanced down at his salt-sprayed sailing clothes. "I guess I'd better get changed." With that, he was gone.

Three hours later, a grand total of four guests had wandered through the library, none of them staying for more than a few minutes. Faith checked the clock. It was past time to shut the library for the day.

"Come on, Watson," she said, closing the doors on the fireplace after stirring the remaining coals so it would burn out. "We might as well go home. Maybe we can stop by the kennels on the way and pay your new girlfriend a visit."

Watson sprang up at that suggestion and bolted to the door.

In the gallery outside the library doors, Brooke surveyed a table of refreshments.

Watson scampered over to her and rubbed against her legs, purring.

Brooke smiled and leaned down to pet him. When she straightened, she gestured to the refreshments. "What do you think?"

Faith regarded the appetizers that resembled such so-called delicacies as eye of newt on a cracker. "They don't look all that appetizing."

Watson meowed as if in agreement.

Brooke grinned. "It's perfect then. That's what Cybil was going for."

Two guests strolled over to the table and helped themselves to the refreshments. Faith couldn't help but overhear their conversation.

"Can you believe the poor woman's death wasn't a hoax?" one woman asked.

The other woman shivered. "No. It's starting to feel as if we're guests at the Bates Motel."

"You don't think she died of natural causes?"

"I'm not sure. Not long before she was found, I saw her and Cybil walking among the topiaries. And there was someone else there too."

Faith gulped at the realization that the woman could be talking about her.

"At the time it didn't seem strange to see a man in the garden," the woman went on. "But now that I think back on it, he appeared to be lurking."

A man? Lurking? Faith's heart raced.

"I think he might have been watching them."

"Did you tell the police? Did you recognize who it was?"

"I told the police, but I don't know who it was. I only glimpsed a figure half-hidden in the foliage and the top of a baseball cap. I'm not sure it was even a man."

Faith sucked in a breath. It couldn't have been her. She hadn't been wearing a hat.

"And there must have been something shiny on the cap," the woman went on, "because at one point, something glinted off it like a beacon. I think that's what caught my attention in the first place."

Marlene's sharp voice echoed off the marble floor. "Faith, could you join us in the salon for a few minutes?" She stood near the salon door with a woman Faith didn't recognize.

"I'll see you later," Faith told Brooke. To Watson, she added, "Stay here. I'll be right back."

Watson wandered over to one of the giant windows overlooking the ocean—which suddenly seemed very choppy.

When Faith walked over to them, Marlene introduced the woman next to her. "This is Tara's mother, Ruth Blue."

Faith shook the woman's hand. "I'm so sorry for your loss," she said, then slanted Marlene a questioning glance.

Marlene didn't explain why she had summoned Faith to join them. Instead, she ushered them into the empty salon. "Let's have a seat in here where it's more private," she said. She led them over to a grouping of chairs, and they all sat down.

"I just came from the morgue," Ruth said without preamble. Her voice broke, but she quickly recovered. "And spoke with the police. But they're wrong."

Faith winced, knowing denial was the first stage of grief. But what was she saying?

"My daughter was murdered," Ruth stated as if she'd read Faith's mind.

Faith stared at her, speechless, even though she knew she should say something. "What makes you so sure?" she finally asked. "The police found no evidence of foul play." She conjured up a figure wearing a baseball cap and lurking in the topiary garden.

"Tara had been acting disturbed lately." Ruth fumbled with the clasp on her purse, then removed a folded note. "And I found this in her things." She pressed the note into Faith's hands.

"'Reporters who can be bought are no better than the scum they whitewash,'" Faith read aloud, stifling a shiver. "The police didn't want to hold on to this and test it for fingerprints?"

"No. They said it didn't prove anything, and they couldn't even know for sure when it was written."

Faith frowned at the plain white printed page. There were tests that could be conducted, but she supposed they would have been too costly and unnecessary, especially if the police didn't believe Tara was murdered.

"Ms. Russell said you might be able to help me," Ruth went on hopefully.

Faith looked from her to Marlene in confusion.

"I told her you seemed to have a bit of a gift for solving mysteries," Marlene said, although her sour expression suggested she wasn't proud of the admission.

Faith didn't know how to respond.

Ruth clasped Faith's arm for a moment. "Please help me convince the police to find the culprit."

"I'm very sorry for your loss, and I would like to help you," Faith said gently. "But I'm afraid the police wouldn't appreciate it if I interfered with their investigation."

"Since when has that ever stopped you?" Marlene asked tartly.

"Please," Ruth repeated. "You know as well as I do that there are all kinds of ways to kill someone undetected. Ways writers like these," she added, gesturing to three chatting female guests who had just walked in, "no doubt spend a great deal of time researching."

The women grinned at Ruth.

"It's our stock-in-trade," one remarked. "Ricin is my personal favorite. It's extremely easy to come by."

"Yes," the woman beside her piped up. "I think I even saw a castor bean tree in the garden here. That's what you derive it from."

"I used insulin to kill one of the victims in my last book," the third woman said. "I asked a coroner once if it would be detectable, and he said it would be a perfect way to do someone in. The only hope he'd have of detecting it would be if he found the puncture wound from the needle."

"Oleander makes a lethal poison too," the second woman interjected. "I noticed a beautiful one in the gallery."

"See?" Ruth said, fluttering her hand toward the women. "Any one of them could have murdered Tara."

The women blanched. "Oh no. We'd never—"

Marlene shot Faith a desperate look as she quickly escorted the guests out of the salon.

"Talking and writing about poisoning someone is a far cry from actually doing it," Faith said to Ruth softly.

"I know. But someone killed her," Ruth insisted.

Faith reread the note Ruth had found in her daughter's belongings and feared she might be right. "Do you know who could have written this?"

"No. And I called her editor, but he didn't know either."

"Perhaps we could figure it out from reading Tara's recent articles. It sounds as if her take on a story annoyed someone." Whether that someone chose to make her pay with her life was another question entirely, but Faith kept that thought to herself.

Wolfe entered the room with the returning Marlene, who had no doubt alerted him to the situation. After introducing himself, Wolfe expressed his sympathy for Ruth's loss. "If we can assist you in any way, please don't hesitate to ask."

"I want you to help me convince the police to keep investigating Tara's death," Ruth said without hesitation. "I know she was murdered. They can't explain how she died, so how can they say it was from natural causes?"

"That's a very good question," Wolfe said. "I'll personally give the police chief a call and see what I can find out. In the meantime, you are more than welcome to stay at the manor. I've asked our concierge vet to bring your daughter's cat up from the kennels for you."

Tears sprang to Ruth's eyes. "Thank you."

"I'll go make that call now. See that Mrs. Blue has everything she needs," Wolfe told Marlene. Then he excused himself.

A few minutes later, Midge and Bill arrived with Midnight. The cat seemed to recognize Ruth on sight and struggled to break free of Midge's hold. She placed her in Ruth's trembling arms, and the cat rubbed her face against Ruth's and purred.

Midge drew Faith aside. "Some of the guests out there are speculating that Tara died of an insulin overdose."

"It was probably because they witnessed Officer Laddy showing the chief a vial and syringes that he discovered in Tara's jacket last night," Faith explained.

"Do you know how much insulin was in the vial?" Midge asked.

"It looked almost full."

"That's good. How many syringes did Laddy find?" Midge persisted.

"I think he said seven," Faith said.

Midge turned to Bill. "Does that sound about right to you?"

"Yeah, she had ten to start, and the cat would have had at least three meals between the time we gave them to her and the time of Tara's death. Even if we're off by one or two, I doubt a cat's dose would be enough to kill a grown woman. Maybe if she'd taken the whole week's supply in one needle."

Midge hushed him and glanced at Tara's mother.

Faith's heart hammered. The last thing Ruth needed was to think he might be suggesting her daughter took her own life.

"Why don't I show you to your daughter's room?" Marlene said to Ruth, sounding as gentle as Faith had ever heard her.

"Yes, that would be nice. Thank you."

"Do you have luggage I can have someone fetch from your car for you?" Marlene asked.

"I can do that," Bill volunteered.

Ruth gave him her car keys. "It's the yellow one, parked just outside."

"We'll wait here for you," Marlene told him.

Watson had apparently picked up Midge's trail when she arrived with Midnight and followed them into the salon. Now he sat on the window ledge, batting at something.

"What have you found?" Faith asked him and walked over to see for herself. "An acorn?"

He knocked it from the ledge, and it bounced off Marlene's shoe.

She snapped it up. "How did this get in here? I need to have a word with housekeeping."

"There's one on every window ledge," Midge pointed out.

"Perhaps it's another one of Cybil's activities," Faith suggested.

Marlene spotted Carrie walking past the door and summoned her. "Do you know if Ms. Crypt is responsible for these acorns?"

The young woman blushed. "No ma'am. I put them on the window ledges."

"Why on earth would you do that?" Marlene demanded.

"Because of what Mr. Jaxon said about Watson licking his fur backward," Carrie said. "That means there's going to be a bad storm, and acorns on the window ledge are supposed to help keep lightning from striking." She dropped her gaze to the floor. "I thought you'd be pleased."

"I'm not. Please collect them. I fail to see how an acorn could possibly prevent lightning from striking the manor." Marlene sniffed. "Besides, I prefer to rely on meteorologists for the forecast instead of cats."

Two bright pink patches bloomed on Carrie's cheeks. "Yes ma'am." She scurried from window to window and gathered up the acorns.

Bill returned with Ruth's suitcases. "I think I grabbed them in the nick of time. It looks like a nasty storm is brewing out there."

Marlene scowled in Carrie's direction as if it were her fault. She motioned Ruth toward the large staircase. "This way, please."

Faith scooped up Watson. "I guess we'd better hurry home before we get caught in the storm."

As Carrie snatched another acorn, a lightning bolt streaked down from the sky, followed by a loud boom.

Everyone sprang to the window.

"Whoa," Carrie whispered.

A large tree had split down the middle, its bark littering the yard around it.

Midge glanced from Carrie to Faith and raised an eyebrow. "Maybe there's something to the superstitions after all?"

"It's a coincidence." Faith groaned, realizing that now she'd have to wait out the storm here with horror writers.

And possibly a murderer.

7

Faith stood at a gallery window watching the angry black clouds piling up in the sky and the distant trees bending in the wind.

A few minutes ago, Watson had trotted up the stairs and disappeared, and Midge and Bill had left for the kennels with one of the attendants. The lightning strike had sent the new mama mare into a frenzy, so the vets had no choice but to brave the severe weather to calm the mare before she injured herself or her foal.

Faith wished there had been enough room for her and Watson to squeeze into the pickup with them so they could have gotten a ride home.

Nolan joined Faith at the window. "Hello again. Will you be sitting in on our panel discussion?"

She shook her head. "I'm just waiting out the storm."

He peered outside as the wind picked up, slashing against the window. "It looks like you'll have quite a wait."

As if on cue, chattering guests started heading toward the salon.

"I love writing during a thunderstorm," one commented. "It gets me in the perfect mood for my stories."

"Something always happens during a thunderstorm," Pierce remarked ominously.

Faith gave an involuntary shudder and hoped Nolan hadn't noticed. These were Tara's fellow writers and possibly her murderer.

"Why don't you join us?" Nolan asked Faith. "You might find it interesting."

Faith decided she should sit in on the discussion since she was here anyway. She thought she might learn something that would help Ruth's cause. She took a fortifying breath. "If you're sure it would be all right."

"Of course. There's plenty of space." Nolan escorted her to the salon and then excused himself to take his place on the panel onstage.

Faith chose a seat in the back row so she could better study the guests. Pierce sat at the end of the row. He'd sat in the back row during her lecture too. She could hear him boasting to another writer about one of his research escapades.

As she let her gaze drift over the guests one by one, she admitted they weren't at all what she'd expected. Faith supposed it had been silly to think that horror writers would be trolling about in Goth or vampire costumes, even if fans of other genres tended to dress up during retreats.

She had a difficult time imagining any of these people being capable of killing Tara. But thanks to their writing research, they all likely had the know-how to get away with murder. And being here at Castleton afforded them the opportunity.

Which left motive as the big question mark. Maybe an author at the retreat was connected to one of the politicians Tara had implicated in her story about mafia-tied bribes.

Wolfe slipped into the seat next to hers. "Are you searching for suspects?"

Faith studied him, a little unnerved that he'd practically read her mind. "That and waiting out the rain."

"I spoke to Chief Garris, and he admitted they don't know how Tara died. But he said he spoke with Tara's editor and learned she'd been depressed lately."

"Depressed, as in suicidal?"

"The editor didn't go that far," Wolfe answered, "but he said if every one of his reporters who received a threatening letter wound up on a slab, not one of them would still be alive."

Faith frowned. "So he doesn't suspect Tara's death has anything to do with the letter Ruth found?"

"I'm sure he doesn't want to believe it does."

"Do you think Tara was murdered?"

"I don't know. We need more facts."

A guest in front of them twisted around and shushed them.

They apologized and fixed their attention on the panel.

The moderator addressed his next question to Nolan. "What do you want in a proposal, and what would earn your immediate rejection?"

"I look for a unique story or a unique angle on a proven trope. And I can't lie—if you have a great platform, it's a tremendous help. Publishers are in the business to make money. So if your best friend is a popular TV network's talk show host who promises to have you on for an interview the week your book releases, then convincing a publisher to take a chance on your book will be much easier for you than for someone without those connections."

The pair sitting in front of Faith grumbled.

"I never thought of it before," Faith whispered to Wolfe, "but it must be hard for writers to cultivate friendships with other writers. I mean, on one hand, they need to network and might genuinely want to help each other succeed. But ultimately they're also in competition for a publisher or agent's limited number of available slots."

Wolfe nodded. "In that case, do you think someone perceived Tara as competition that needed to be taken out?"

Faith replayed in her mind what Tara had said about her writing aspirations as Midge and Bill examined her cat. "I didn't get the impression she'd even finished her first novel."

The door squeaked open, and Carrie entered with a tray of cheese and crackers. She glanced around the room, then headed toward the refreshment table at the side wall.

"What kind of manuscript would you reject outright?" the moderator asked Nolan.

"A plagiarized one," Nolan said firmly and without hesitation. "In my mind, a writer can't sink any lower than to try to pass off someone else's work as his or her own."

Murmurs rippled across the room.

Faith whispered to Wolfe, "When I worked at Hawarden University, one of the professors constantly did online searches to see if the students had plagiarized their essays. It's far too easy to get away with it."

Cybil raised her hand, and when the moderator acknowledged her, she asked, "Has a plagiarized work actually crossed your desk?"

Nolan nodded. "I recently judged a contest for aspiring writers, and one of the submissions was clearly a thinly veiled plagiarism of a story from Pierce Baltimore's newest release."

Faith heard a sharp intake of breath.

Carrie stood as if frozen, staring at the stage.

"How this writer could think such a blatant copy wouldn't be recognized is beyond me," Nolan went on.

As Faith continued to watch Carrie, she noticed the young housekeeper's attention shift to Pierce.

Then Carrie fumbled the tray. Cheese and crackers slid off the edge. In her attempt to recover it, she overcompensated and sent the whole tray clattering to the floor.

Cybil jumped up. "What did you see?" she asked Carrie, sounding nervous.

Faith noticed that Cybil subtly jutted her chin toward the curtains behind the stage. So Carrie's clumsiness had been an act. Faith wondered what kind of prank they were pulling. *It seems a little insensitive since someone just died during the last one.*

Carrie pointed a shaky finger to the stage. "Something's behind the curtain."

Heads swiveled in the direction she indicated, but at that moment, the lights snapped off.

An uproar ensued. Faith and Wolfe surged to their feet. Guests lit up their cell phone screens, trying to make out what was happening.

Then the lights blinked back on, and a figure raced from the stage.

"Who was that?" someone asked.

Cybil, now at the doorway, called out, "He went down the stairs."

Some of the guests left the room in pursuit while most of them milled around, talking.

Faith walked over to the refreshment table. Carrie was gone. *She's probably dying of embarrassment.* When Faith bent down to pick up the cheese and crackers Carrie had spilled, she spotted the tip of a shoe, which jerked under the long tablecloth.

Faith lifted the cloth and found Carrie cowering under the table. "Did Cybil put you up to this?"

She hugged her knees to her chest. "Sort of."

"Come on out. We need to clean up this mess before Marlene wonders what all the ruckus is about."

Watson twined around Faith's legs and then did his bit to pitch in by eating some of the cheese.

By the time Faith finished helping Carrie, Cybil had come clean on the practical joke.

Most of the guests chuckled over their reactions, and some claimed they knew it all along.

Faith went over to Wolfe. "I'm relieved the prank was pretty tame. Being Friday the thirteenth, I was worried we might be in for something gruesome."

"The night is still young," he said.

Faith shivered. "In that case, I think it's time to go home. The rain seems to have let up."

"Wait a minute. Didn't you get my message?"

"Message?" Faith pulled out her cell phone and glanced at the screen. "No, sorry. I missed it." Sure enough, she had an unopened text from him.

"The bookdealer is coming in"—Wolfe checked his watch—"fifty minutes to show us the books."

"Fifty minutes! We still haven't reviewed the list."

"We can do that now." Wolfe led her up to his office on the third floor.

Remembering the delicious salmon she hadn't gotten the chance to finish the last time she'd been invited upstairs, she wondered if he'd order them up dinner this evening too. The guests would be going for theirs shortly. Her stomach grumbled.

"I'll make us tea while you get started," Wolfe said.

Mortified that he must have heard her gastronomical entreaty, she sank into a chair and thanked him.

He shifted his laptop to face her and tapped in his password for her, then handed her the dealer's printout. "I'll be right back." A few minutes later, he returned with a plate of shortbread cookies and two cups of tea. "This should tide us over through the meeting."

Helping herself to a cookie, Faith launched a search on the next book on the dealer's list.

Forty-five minutes later, she jotted down an estimated value for the last book on the list. "That's all of them."

Wolfe's phone beeped, and he glanced at the screen. "Perfect timing. Our bookdealer has arrived." He grimaced at his phone screen. "It seems he's been wandering around the manor for some time, trying to make his way to my apartment. Let's go down and meet him."

They took the elevator to the main floor. A short, rumpled man with a large briefcase at his feet was waiting in the lobby.

Faith eyed the man, who'd apparently had no qualms about making himself at home and exploring the manor. He seemed vaguely familiar.

"Faith, this is Ronald Adams, the bookdealer I was telling you about," Wolfe said. "Ronald, this is Castleton's librarian, Faith Newberry."

The man removed his baseball cap and extended his hand.

"You seem familiar," Faith said, shaking his hand. "Have we met before?"

"I don't think so."

"Do you live in Lighthouse Bay?"

Ronald seemed oddly taken aback by the question. "No ma'am. I'm from Providence."

Faith frowned, certain she'd seen him somewhere before.

"You might have seen him here last night," Wolfe suggested. "I wasn't able to get in touch with him to cancel our appointment before he was already on his way."

"Oh, that must be it," Faith said.

"Shall we take a look at the books?" Wolfe asked, then led the way to the library.

When they entered the room, Ronald set the briefcase on the table and spread out his wares.

"Did you bring cotton gloves for handling the books?" Faith asked, not wanting to get the oils from her hands on them.

"Sorry, no. But you can handle them."

Faith shot Wolfe a questioning glance. This man clearly wasn't experienced in handling rare books. "That's all right. I have some here."

She put on the gloves and then carefully examined each book. Sadly, the books were largely unimpressive. Ronald had listed several of the books as first editions, but only two actually were, and they weren't the ones on her wish list. She had to wonder why the man was wasting their time.

"I'm afraid that none of these copies are truly up to Castleton Manor's standards." Faith knew it sounded snooty, but the man was either a total neophyte when it came to rare books or he was trying to bamboozle them.

"Yes, I have to agree with Miss Newberry," Wolfe added. "I'd hoped to acquire *To Kill a Mockingbird* at the very least, but your sample is nothing more than a mass market copy I could pick up at any secondhand store." There was a slight edge in his tone.

"I understand. They're not for everyone," Ronald conceded as he collected the books and returned them to his briefcase. Then, in true salesman style, he added, "If you'd like to give me a wish list, I'd be happy to watch for the books you want."

"I appreciate the offer," Wolfe said, "but I think I'll pass."

Ronald held up his hands. "Okay, I won't argue. The customer is always right. I'll be going now."

Wolfe stood. "We'll walk with you."

"I'll see myself out." The man waved off the offer and clicked his briefcase shut.

"I insist," Wolfe said firmly.

Faith hid a smile. Wolfe obviously didn't trust the bookdealer. Given how Ronald had been wandering around the manor, Faith had to wonder if he had fabricated the quality of his stock in order to gain an appointment and therefore an opportunity to case the estate. He'd evidently expected to meet Wolfe in his private apartment too—the one area of the manor not open to the public.

What had Ronald Adams actually wanted at Castleton Manor?

8

By the time Faith and Wolfe had escorted the bookdealer to the door, the retreat guests were filtering down the stairs from their after-dinner break. Cybil was answering questions and directing guests to the salon, where a horror movie was scheduled to be shown.

"Give me a moment to grab an umbrella, and I'll walk you home," Wolfe said.

"That's not necessary," Faith protested.

"Yes, it is. I kept you past dinner and past dark. It's the least I can do." Wolfe strode away.

Faith called Watson, who traipsed over to her with his new girlfriend.

Ruth hurried after the pair and scooped Midnight up. "You're leaving?" she asked Faith, sounding concerned.

"Yes, I need to get home to feed Watson and make my own dinner."

"I just assumed you had a room here too."

"I have a cottage on the estate."

"Oh, good. Then you'll be back tomorrow?" Ruth hugged Midnight to her chest. "I've been going through Tara's notebooks, and I have questions about the people she made note of since arriving here."

"I'd be happy to help you with that in the morning," Faith assured her.

Wolfe returned with an umbrella and started to guide Faith to the door, Watson following.

"Wait," Pierce called from halfway down the main staircase.

Wolfe glanced over his shoulder. "Are you talking to me?"

Pierce slowed and held the bannister in a white-knuckle grip. "You're the owner, right?"

"Yes. Is there a problem?"

Pierce descended the remaining stairs and stumbled over to them, his face ashen. He thrust out his hand, a note crumpled in his fingers. "Someone slipped this under my door when I was at dinner."

Wolfe took it from him and unfolded it.

"What does it say?" Faith asked.

"'You're next,'" Wolfe read out loud. He showed them the note, the words typed in a large font.

Carrie, who had also apparently delayed going home because of the storm, yelped. She pointed to Pierce's name tag. "His name is written in red ink."

Faith glanced at the name tags of other attendees and realized Pierce's was the only one in red. Perhaps it was because he was their main speaker for Sunday's book signing event, which was open to the public.

"If you write a person's name in red ink it means they will die soon," Carrie said, her voice quavering.

"It's true," murmured one of the guests who was standing nearby.

Cybil strolled up and said, "I'm so sorry. My black marker ran out of ink. I'm sure it doesn't mean anything." Then she tilted her head as if listening for something. "Do you hear that?"

"What?" Faith asked.

"I hear a bell tolling," Cybil said melodramatically. "Doesn't anyone else hear it?" Her voice rose in panic, and she appeared deeply concerned.

The people around them shook their heads.

Nolan chuckled as he joined them.

"This is no joking matter," Pierce snapped.

"Yes, why would you laugh?" Faith asked, feeling like she was missing a significant inside joke.

"If you hear a tolling bell and no one else does, it means someone will die," Nolan explained. "It was in Pierce's book."

Ah. So if Cybil was making fun of the note, she must not think it was real. Was it just another prank?

Ruth gestured to the note. "This proves Tara was murdered."

A guest pointed at Carrie. "I saw that housekeeper sneaking around upstairs earlier with a note in her hand."

Carrie shot a panicked glance at Cybil.

"We don't want to miss the movie that will be starting in the salon soon," Cybil said to the loitering guests. "Please follow me." She swiftly ushered them away.

"We need to call the police," Ruth insisted when Cybil returned.

"No. I can explain," Cybil told Ruth. "The note isn't real. I'd planned to follow up what was supposed to be Tara's feigned demise with the note, and I forgot to tell Carrie not to deliver it after Tara . . ." Her voice trailed off, and then she added, "I'm so sorry for causing you additional distress." Cybil shot Pierce a look that said she wasn't sorry about his distress.

Carrie pulled a piece of paper from her pocket. "But I didn't deliver your note."

Cybil snatched the paper from Carrie's hand. As she examined it, the blood drained from her face too. "This is the note I wrote. That one looks like it was typed."

On impulse, Faith glanced at Nolan, who hadn't wandered off with the rest of the group to watch the movie. If he'd found out about the aborted practical joke, given his grudge against Pierce, she could see him reinstituting it himself. Yet he didn't seem amused by Cybil's anxiety.

Then Faith looked at Pierce. She imagined that he would enjoy turning the tables on Cybil, but he still seemed deeply disturbed as well. That could mean only one thing—someone had slipped the note under Pierce's door. Someone who'd meant it.

Wolfe pulled out his cell phone and called the police. "Can someone please shut off that ridiculous music?"

Throughout the day Cybil had ensured that eerie theme music from such horror classics as *Jaws* and *Psycho* was piped into the manor's common areas in a continuous mind-numbing loop. Faith had long since managed to tune it out. Now she hurried to the control panel and switched it off.

Clicking off his phone, Wolfe said, "The police will send someone over as soon as they can, but since it's not an emergency, it didn't sound as if it would be right away." To Faith, he said, "I can walk you home now."

Faith nibbled on her bottom lip, her gaze drifting from a clearly distraught Carrie to Pierce, Cybil, and finally to Ruth. If she went home now, she'd only wonder all night about what the police would say about the note. "I think I'd like to stay until the police arrive. I'll just slip down to the kitchen for a few minutes to see if I can scrounge up a plate of leftovers for supper."

Watson meowed.

She smiled. "Yes, I'll look for something for you too," she told him.

"If you'd like to go and watch your movie," Wolfe said to the others, "I can let you know when the police arrive."

Pierce shook his head and paced. "I can't sit and watch a movie now."

"I'm going to quickly drop by the salon to make sure the movie started," Cybil said, "and then I'll wait out here too."

"May I go home?" Carrie asked.

"Yes," Wolfe said. "If the police have any questions for you, I'll let them know you'll be back in the morning. By the way, did you see anyone else outside Mr. Baltimore's room or wandering the halls when you were up there?"

"A guest or two went into their rooms," Carrie answered. "And there was a short man with a briefcase trying to find his way to the third floor. He said he was a bookdealer and he had an appointment with you, so I led him down to the front desk to wait for you. I hope that was okay."

"You did the right thing," Wolfe told her. "Thank you."

"Where was this bookdealer from?" Nolan asked.

"Providence," Wolfe answered. "Why do you ask?"

Nolan smirked at Pierce. "Did you tick off a bookdealer in Providence?"

Pierce looked down his nose at Nolan. "No. I've never been asked to do a signing there."

Faith pulled Wolfe aside. "The bookdealer was here last night when Tara died too." Ronald Adams had struck her as suspicious from the moment she saw him in the lobby, and the unsuitableness of his collection of books had only solidified the impression. "What do you know about him?"

"Not much," Wolfe admitted. "He approached me while I was having lunch in town last week and asked how I was enjoying the book I was reading. We struck up a conversation about books. He seemed knowledgeable on the subject. When he learned who I was, he claimed he'd heard about the manor's library and might have some books I'd be interested in acquiring, so I told him to e-mail me a list."

Wolfe was a seasoned businessman and unlikely to be easily duped, but as reluctant as she was to suggest it, Faith doubted that the bookdealer had just happened to strike up a conversation with Wolfe.

As if he knew what she was thinking, Wolfe shook his head. "Ronald may have had designs to case the place, but I doubt his intentions had to do with any of our guests. We bumped into each other more than a week ago. The chances of me inviting him here at the same time Tara and Pierce were here were pretty slim."

"Unless he carefully timed the delivery of the list, planning to show up with his briefcase of books whether he'd heard from you or not. He was wearing a baseball cap, just like the person lurking in the topiary garden."

"What person lurking in the garden?"

Faith related the conversation she had overheard and how one of the guests had spotted a figure in the topiary garden before Tara died.

Wolfe bounced the umbrella he was carrying against the side of his leg. "I think I'll take a walk around the manor and through the parking lot to ensure our bookdealer has vacated the premises."

"Then again," Faith said, rethinking her theory, "how would Ronald have known which room Pierce was in?" She realized she really had let her imagination run away with her. "And what could his motive be for targeting them?"

"Learning the room would have been easy enough, but I'm not sure about motive," Wolfe admitted. "It might not be connected to our retreat guests, but I'm still going to go check outside." He marched out the door.

Faith headed downstairs to the kitchen, Watson at her heels.

"Hey, what are you still doing here?" Brooke tossed her apron into the laundry hamper. "I was going to stop by your place on my way out." She opened a small container and showed Faith the contents. "I thought you might like to sample these chocolate-and-cream cheese cupcakes. I promise there are no eyeballs inside."

Faith grinned. "Glad to hear it. Are there any appendage-free entrées left over too?"

Brooke opened the fridge and rooted around. "You don't want to cook tonight?"

"I won't be going home for a while," Faith said, then explained what had happened.

"Are you serious?" Brooke scooped potatoes, vegetables, and chicken parmigiana onto a plate. "I'll stick around with you. Maybe we can solve this mystery before the police get here."

Faith pulled up a stool to the counter and sat down. "If the note writer killed Tara like her mother assumes, are you sure you want to risk a run-in with him?"

Brooke popped the plate of leftovers into the microwave. "I think someone's just messing with Pierce. If you haven't noticed, he isn't very nice."

"Maybe."

The microwave beeped, and Brooke set the piping hot plate in front of Faith.

Watson twined around Brooke's legs, meowing loudly.

"I suppose you want something too? You know you're not supposed to be in here," Brooke said sweetly.

Watson blinked up at her innocently.

Brooke pulled a tin of tuna from the cupboard and opened it. Then she scraped the tuna onto a disposable plate and set it down just outside the kitchen door for the cat. "I hear we have Watson to thank for this storm."

Faith groaned. "Please tell me you don't believe those superstitions."

Brooke shrugged. "They seem to keep coming true."

Faith dug into her dinner, not wanting to debate Brooke's logic.

"Maybe I should bring Diva and Bling in with me tomorrow," Brooke mused. "If the note writer is still here, they'll know who he is. They can spot jerks a mile away. They go into a swimming frenzy at the sight of them or at the sound of their voice."

Diva and Bling were Brooke's angelfish, and while Faith wouldn't give them credit for half the intelligence Brooke did, she wasn't about to crush Brooke by saying so. Besides, given the lack of evidence in this case, unless the police found fingerprints on that note, Brooke's fish might be their best shot at finding the guy.

Faith's cell phone beeped with a text from Wolfe: *Chief Garris is here in the billiard room.*

She quickly finished her meal and tucked the container with the cupcakes into her bag.

Watson raced Faith and Brooke upstairs, then wandered away when they reached the lobby.

Midge burst through the main door. "What's going on? As I was leaving the stables after checking on the new foal, I saw a police cruiser drive in."

Faith pulled her aside and whispered, "Someone slid a note under Pierce Baltimore's door that said, 'You're next.' Chief Garris is questioning some of the guests in the billiard room."

"Sit in with us," Brooke urged. "If we all put our heads together, we should be able to figure out what's going on."

They slipped into the room and joined Wolfe, Chief Garris, Pierce, Cybil, Nolan, and Ruth. Thankfully Marlene had gone home early, or the tension in the room would have been even higher.

Chief Garris scanned the group. "Did you see anyone near Mr. Baltimore's room?"

"I saw that male vet wandering up on the second floor earlier," Cybil replied.

"The vet is Bill Stephenson," Midge said sharply, "and he went upstairs to check on Midnight at my request." She explained to the chief why Bill was working with her for a few days.

"Has anyone ever threatened you before?" Garris asked Pierce.

"Yeah, too many times to count. I just never believed any of them until now." Pierce raked his fingers through his hair. "Fans are crazy. If they don't like the way you kill off a favorite character, suddenly you're public enemy number one."

"A few of his editors have uttered death threats too," Nolan quipped.

Cybil laughed.

Brooke whispered to Faith, "I've heard Pierce is a bit of a prima donna to work with."

"Do you have family?" the chief asked Pierce.

"I'm divorced, and the ex gets a healthy alimony that would dry up if I died. No children."

"You make a good income as a writer?"

Pierce glanced at Cybil and smirked. "Better than most."

Chief Garris seemed to make note of the interplay as well as Pierce's answer before continuing. "And what did you do before you started writing full-time?"

"I was an army medic." Pierce sat a little straighter as if subconsciously reacting to a drill sergeant's command.

"Did you make any enemies in the military?"

"Nope, never lost a soldier. At least not any that weren't already beyond saving."

Garris nodded and made another note.

"Aren't you going to ask him why someone would want to kill him and my daughter?" Ruth demanded.

The chief's expression was empathetic. "We don't know that the note writer killed your daughter."

Ruth twisted the tissue she held in her hands. "It sure sounds to me like he's taking credit for it."

"All the toxicology screens have come back negative," Garris said.

So they had no evidence Tara was murdered.

Ruth clenched her fists. "Did the coroner search her body for puncture marks?" She blinked several times, clearly attempting to stave off a fresh bout of tears. "I read somewhere that they'll inject in inconspicuous places, like between the toes. Did you check between her toes?"

"I'll have to ask the coroner about that."

Pierce pushed to his feet. "If we're done here, I'm checking out and going home."

"You can't leave," Cybil said. "You said you'd give the tribute to Tara tomorrow morning after breakfast. And all your fans are counting on seeing you Sunday afternoon."

Pierce shrugged. "They'll understand."

"I wouldn't be so sure," Nolan said, leaning back in his chair. "All you'll do is make more people mad at you."

"If your note writer is a psychotic fan," the chief interrupted, "you'd be safer here, where we can be on the lookout for him."

"The guy might want you to run so he can get you alone," Cybil added.

"I'm not going to stick around and be bait," Pierce insisted.

"Do you think the threat will just go away if you leave?" Wolfe asked.

That question gave Pierce pause. "Okay, okay, I'll stick around." He faced the chief. "But your men had better catch this guy."

9

Bored with waiting for his person to finish talking so they could return to the cottage, the cat padded around the manor in search of something intriguing to do. He heard odd squeals and yelps drifting from the room with the flickering lights, so he pushed the door open far enough to slip inside.

The smell of melted butter made his stomach growl. Weaving around the humans' legs, he found all sorts of buttery white puffs and stopped to lick one before moving on. The humans were so busy watching the moving picture on the wall that they were spilling the tasty treats left, right, and center.

It was hard to enjoy the puffs, though, thanks to the annoying sounds bouncing around the room. At first he thought it was from furniture being scraped across the floor, which was always fun because humans didn't clean under furniture much and he could usually find something interesting left behind.

Instead, he traced the sound to a contraption with a flickering light at the back of the room and went to investigate.

The room darkened, and the humans went into an uproar.

"Get that cat away from the projector!" one of the humans shouted.

Another human plucked the cat from the table and plopped him outside the door.

The nerve! The cat swiped at the person's ankle.

The human nudged him away with the toe of his shoe.

The human with the baubles on her neck click-clacked down the hall. "Is everything set for tonight?" she whispered.

The cat arched his back and rubbed his fur against her calf, hoping she'd replenish her pocket with more fish treats.

The human behind the noisy contraption, who'd thrown him out of the room, nodded. "The housekeeper planted the stuff like we told her and"—he patted his pocket—"the batteries are charged."

"Perfect," she said, stooping down and giving the cat's neck an agreeable rub. "I'll give you the signal about twenty minutes after the last light goes out. People have been keyed up all night, expecting the other shoe to drop, but by then . . ."

Her partner grinned. "They won't know what hit them."

Long after Chief Garris left with Pierce's threatening note, Faith lingered in the billiard room, exchanging ideas with Brooke, Midge, Wolfe, and Ruth as to why someone might target both Pierce and Tara.

"They've got to be connected somehow," Ruth insisted.

"We already know a few ways they're connected," Faith said. She counted them off on her fingers. "They're both members of the same group of horror writers. Tara interviewed Pierce for a magazine article. And the morning Tara died, they had a heated discussion in the garden."

"About what?" Brooke asked.

"I don't know," Faith replied. "I didn't think it was any of my business at the time. I wish I'd thought of it while the chief was here. I would have brought it up so he could have asked Pierce."

"We should ask him right now," Midge said. "After all, Pierce doesn't want to be this guy's next victim, and if his last conversation with Tara might offer a clue to identifying him, Pierce shouldn't mind being asked about it."

Somehow Faith suspected Pierce would mind a great deal, but she followed Midge up the stairs anyway.

"Which room is he in?" Midge asked.

"The Arthur Conan Doyle Suite."

Midge rapped on the door.

"Who is it?" Pierce asked.

Midge signaled to Faith to respond.

"It was your idea to talk to him," Faith argued quietly.

"But he knows you better."

Faith narrowed her eyes at her friend but called out, "Faith Newberry. I have a question that might help us identify your note writer."

The door opened. "You think you know who it is?" Pierce asked eagerly.

"Well, if he already killed Tara as his note implies," Faith answered, "it would seem that his motive is connected to something the two of you share or have done together."

Pierce frowned. "I scarcely knew the woman. She interviewed me for an article a few months ago, and that was the extent of our contact."

"Not quite," Faith said. "The two of you had a rather heated conversation the other morning. What was that about?"

An emotion Faith couldn't identify flitted across Pierce's face. "I can't recall."

"Try," Midge urged. "If it was the last interaction the two of you had before she died, it could be significant."

Pierce's frown deepened, his brows furrowing. "I'm sorry. But I can't remember."

"We apologize for disturbing you," Faith said, and she prodded Midge toward the stairs.

"I don't believe him," Midge whispered. "He's probably more worried that whatever they talked about might get out than the possibility it is somehow tied to a killer."

"What did Pierce say?" Brooke asked as Faith and Midge returned to the billiard room.

"He claims he doesn't remember," Midge said.

"Maybe the note Tara received was about her interview with

Pierce," Ruth theorized. "Remember? 'Reporters who can be bought are no better than the scum they whitewash.'"

"Pierce may be egotistical," Wolfe said, "but 'scum' seems like a stretch."

"I read the article Tara wrote about him," Faith said. "It basically talked about his publishing history, accolades, and awards, then relayed his answers to her interview questions about how he researches his books. I can't see what she would have been guilty of whitewashing or how he would have bought her."

"Maybe he offered to endorse her first novel," Brooke said. "That would have been a huge coup."

"In return for what?" Faith asked. "The story was nothing more than a typical celebrity interview."

"Sure, but we don't know what she left out," Brooke said. "That's where the whitewash could come in."

Ruth rummaged through her bag. "I have Tara's handwritten notes from that interview right here. After I saw the note, I collected all her notebooks from her apartment to bring to the police." She pulled a spiral notebook from the bag and flipped through the pages. "Here it is." She skimmed through the four pages of notes. "She seems to have reported what he said verbatim."

"What if the note you found in your daughter's belongings has nothing to do with her death?" Wolfe ventured. "If the killer was here solely to target Mr. Baltimore, then Miss Blue might have simply gotten in the way. Wasn't there an incident in the library involving Mr. Baltimore?"

"That's right," Faith said. "And it was before Tara's death. A bookcase almost fell on Pierce. I doubt it could have killed him, but I did notice an odd indentation in the rug that made me suspect someone had wedged a doorstop or something similarly shaped under one corner to deliberately make the bookcase unstable."

"Maybe Tara saw who pushed it or who put the wedge under the corner and put two and two together," Brooke speculated.

With the talk of books, Faith thought about the coincidental timing of the bookdealer's visits to the manor. "If the bookcase incident is connected to the threat and Tara's death, I guess that would eliminate our bookdealer unless he snuck onto the estate even before we realized," she said to Wolfe.

"What bookdealer?" Midge and Brooke asked in unison.

Wolfe explained Ronald Adams's visit and their suspicion that it had been a pretense to gain entry to the manor to case the place. Or even worse, perhaps he had arrived to target Tara and Pierce.

"Have you ever heard Tara mention a man name Ronald Adams?" Faith asked Ruth.

Ruth shook her head.

"And Pierce didn't seem concerned about the threat of a bookdealer when Nolan suggested it," Wolfe recalled.

"But maybe he isn't a bookdealer at all. He could be posing as one." Faith pulled up a search engine on her smartphone and typed in the man's name.

A website for a bookstore in Providence appeared, but then again, websites were easy enough to fabricate to give potential marks an illusion of legitimacy.

Faith did a search on the website. "Okay, his website has been around for six years, so if he's pulling a con, it's a long-standing one."

"I can ask the chief to do a background check on him," Wolfe said. "But given the bookcase incident, I think it's safe to assume that Ronald is not connected to Tara's death or the threat to Pierce."

"So supposing Tara only became a target because of something she saw," Midge said, "who wants Pierce dead and has the wherewithal to murder Tara without leaving any evidence?"

This reminded Faith of an earlier conversation about research. A writer had explained that she used insulin to kill off a character in her book. "One of the writers said that using insulin to murder someone can be hard to detect."

"Well, Nolan is diabetic," Brooke informed them. "We have to make his desserts sugar-free."

"He wouldn't hurt Tara," Ruth objected. "They were good friends. And he's been very sweet to me since I arrived."

But he loathes Pierce. In Faith's mind, Ruth's observations could just as easily be construed as strikes against him. Since they were friends, Tara wouldn't have hesitated to call Nolan on his so-called gag in the library. But if he planned to escalate them over the course of the weekend, he might have feared her interference would ruin everything.

"I'm always hesitant to trust the charmers," Midge said softly, no doubt thinking along the same lines as Faith.

"There's no harm in talking to him," Wolfe declared. "If Nolan is as eager to help Ruth as he claims, he should be more than willing to answer our questions."

Nolan peeked in the doorway. "Did I hear my name?"

"Yes." Wolfe waved him in. "We'd like to ask you a few questions."

"Certainly." Nolan sailed into the room and sat beside Ruth. He clasped her hand and gave it a gentle squeeze. "How are you holding up?"

Tears sprang to her eyes. "I'm okay. Thank you."

He gave her hand another squeeze and turned his attention to Wolfe.

"Where were you at the time of Tara's death?" Wolfe asked.

"As I told the police," Nolan said, "I was meeting with one of my clients on the loggia. At least that's where we were when we heard all the commotion. Before my meeting, I wandered around the gardens for a few minutes. But I'm afraid I didn't see Tara."

"You don't like Pierce very much, do you?" Wolfe asked bluntly.

Nolan chuckled. "I enjoy poking fun at him because he's so easy to rile. If you're asking whether I resent him enough to send him that note, the answer is no. He may have dumped me as his agent, but as long as he's alive and kicking and attracting new readers who will eventually check out his backlist, I still make money off him."

Wolfe nodded.

"Now Cybil," Nolan went on. "She has a great deal of resentment against Pierce. You got a glimpse of it during your lecture in the library," he said to Faith. "And I can tell you that she's never happy when he gets more press than she does, so she could have held that against Tara when she interviewed Pierce."

A gasp at the doorway drew everyone's attention.

Cybil stood there, glaring daggers at Nolan. "How could you say such a thing?"

Faith bit her bottom lip, trying to decide if this was another of Cybil's acts. After all, she'd had opportunity. Faith had seen her with Tara shortly before her death. Not to mention Cybil was the one who'd set up the whole topiary prank.

Brooke raised her hand. "I have a question. How could anyone have known where Pierce would be sitting in the library to rig the bookcase ahead of time?"

Cybil fluttered her hand. "Anyone who attends our writers meetings knows Pierce always sits in the back right-hand corner of a room."

Everyone was silent for a long moment.

Cybil looked around the room, her gaze momentarily resting on each person. "I swear to you I did not hurt Tara. And I have no idea who did or what happened. When I left her near the topiary, she didn't appear physically distressed in any way. And I can't imagine anyone wanting to hurt her."

"What about Pierce?" Faith asked.

Cybil crossed her arms. "I openly admit that I don't share a good opinion of Pierce. He may be a popular author with the public, but he is utterly self-absorbed and not well-liked by anyone who really knows him." She nodded at Nolan. "Especially his former agent."

"This finger-pointing isn't constructive," Wolfe cut in.

Midge glanced at her watch. "I'd better get going. Peter and Atticus haven't seen much of me during the past few days. By the time I got home yesterday, Atticus had unraveled the sleeve of his doggy sweater."

Faith hid a smile at the mental image of Midge's Chihuahua chewing on the latest addition to his wardrobe. Midge had taken to doting on the dog to cope with her empty nest, and her husband, Peter, handled the situation by playing bass in a classic rock-and-roll band.

Brooke rose and stretched. "Me too. Diva and Bling hate it when I'm out late." To Faith, she added, "Want a lift home?"

"That would be great. Just give me a minute to round up Watson." She called him and waited, but he didn't come running. "Maybe he slipped outside when someone opened the door." Faith called outside.

Still nothing.

"That's strange." Thinking he might have gone to the kitchen to search for more food, she wandered down to the basement, calling his name.

"Faith," Wolfe called down the back stairs, "I found him."

Faith raced up the stairs to find Wolfe standing outside the butler's pantry, cuddling Watson.

"The door of the pantry was closed, and he was trapped inside," Wolfe said.

Watson's disgruntled mew made Faith's heart miss a beat, because it wasn't like Watson to get himself stuck inside a room. In fact, if she were to hazard a guess, someone did it to him.

But who? And why?

10

Before climbing into bed, Faith opened the bedroom window to chase the stale air from the cottage. The storm seemed to have left the outside air smelling extra fresh. She wagged a finger at Watson. "Now no sitting on the window ledge and yowling at the moon."

The cat curled up at the foot of her bed, as if such an activity were the last thing that would interest him.

Faith woke with a start and squinted at her bedside clock. It was midnight. Then she faced the window, expecting to see Watson, but he wasn't there.

He lazily stretched a leg where he still lay at the foot of her bed. He clearly hadn't woke her.

Faith stared at him. "It wasn't you?" She put on slippers and padded to the window. As she watched, the lights in the second-story suites at the manor began to switch on. Her stomach clenched, and she wondered what was going on now.

Watson jumped onto the window ledge and stared out too. Then he hopped down and dashed to the bedroom door, glancing at her over his shoulder as if to say, "Are you coming?"

"I'm the librarian," she told him. "Whatever is going on at the manor right now has nothing to do with me."

The cat padded a few more steps away and looked back at her again.

"Okay, okay. I won't be able to sleep now anyway. I'll be too worried about what's going on. Give me a minute to change."

Watson sat down as if satisfied with her acquiescence.

Faith quickly dressed and grabbed a flashlight. The idea of crossing through the topiary garden in the dead of night on Friday the thirteenth—although she supposed it was technically Saturday now—didn't sound particularly appealing. "Let's follow the driveway."

She jogged along the gravel driveway while Watson took the shortcut. By the time she reached the terrace, he was already sitting there, peeking in through the French doors.

Faith cupped her hands around her eyes and peered through the glass, but she couldn't see anything because the first floor was still shrouded in darkness.

Faith unlocked the door, and Watson scampered inside ahead of her.

Muffled voices, some angry, carried down the stairs.

Faith raced up to the second floor and joined the group crammed into the corridor. "What happened?"

"Another of Cybil's tricks," a blond-haired man said, sounding beyond aggravated.

"Hey," Cybil protested. "The retreat description said you'd be given a taste of the horror novels you love to read and write."

"Sure," the man retorted, "but the opportunity to sleep would be nice too."

"Yeah," a young woman piped up. "If I wanted to be kept up all night, I could have stayed home with my teething one-year-old."

Wolfe held up his hand, effectively silencing the disgruntled guests. He wore sweatpants and a Boston Red Sox T-shirt, and his hair was mussed. Obviously he'd been asleep too. "May I suggest that we have a moratorium on any pranks between ten at night and eight in the morning?"

Votes of agreement rose from the group.

Wolfe looked to Cybil. "Agreed?"

She shrugged. "Whatever."

"Great," Wolfe said. "What do you say we all get some sleep now?"

The guests muttered and shuffled off to their rooms.

Faith waited until the hall was almost clear before approaching Wolfe. "What was the caper this time?"

"Cybil had one of the housekeepers hide remote-controlled MP3 players in a few of the rooms. Then once all the lights were out, she played whistling."

"Whistling?" Faith repeated.

Wolfe smiled. "According to one of Pierce's stories, hearing whistling in your sleep means snakes will come in."

"I don't think I want to know the rest."

Wolfe chuckled. "She used rubber snakes. They sprang out when the bedside lamps were turned on."

"Cybil certainly went to a lot of trouble to set up all these pranks."

"She had a compatriot, the photographer. Jonathan is also an electronics geek by the sound of it," Wolfe said. "Come on. I'll walk you home."

Faith protested that it wasn't necessary, but Wolfe insisted. She glanced around. "Watson is around here somewhere too."

At the mention of his name, he proudly trotted around the corner, a rubber snake dangling from his mouth.

"Hail to the conquering victor," Wolfe joked.

Faith laughed.

Jonathan rounded the corner after Watson. When he saw Faith and Wolfe, he said, "I can't keep that cat away from the snakes. I'm just glad he didn't ruin the stunt."

His comment reminded Faith of something. "Earlier he was trapped inside the pantry. Do you have any idea what happened?"

Jonathan gave her a sheepish expression. "I'm sorry about that. He was running off with the snakes, so I closed the door when he hid in the pantry. I was going to let him out as soon as everything was set up, but when I went back, he was already gone."

Well, that was one mystery solved. The pranksters had tried to keep Watson from letting the snakes out of the bag too soon, so to speak.

Watson sat down, dropped the snake, and proceeded to groom himself.

Jonathan retrieved the snake, then said good night and headed to his room.

Wolfe led the way downstairs with Watson trailing. "This reminds me of the time I snuck a snake into my brother's bed," he mused.

"A real one?" Faith asked.

"Of course."

Faith shuddered. "I guess I should be thankful I only had a sister. She thinks cats are creepy and shouldn't be in the house, so I never had to worry she'd bring in something like a snake."

"Or a toad. Or a slug." The amusement in Wolfe's voice told her he and his brothers had done it all.

"You must have driven your mom crazy."

He grinned.

Faith didn't usually work on weekends, but she returned to the manor later that morning. She was surprised to see a horseshoe propped up against a terrace step. "I think Carrie has been hard at work attempting to counter all the bad vibes this group is giving off," Faith said to Watson.

When she walked through the door, she was greeted by ocean sounds piping through the sound system instead of the scary theme music. She was going to comment on this to Watson, but when she looked down, he was already scampering away.

Cybil breezed over and gave her a silver charm of a four-leaf clover. "This is for you. A good-luck charm."

"That's okay. Thank you," Faith said, handing it back to her. "Save it for your group."

"No, I insist. I have plenty. Consider it a peace offering." She held it out.

Faith accepted it, but she couldn't help wondering what Cybil's ulterior motives were. It felt like the retreat was being turned upside down.

"Pierce will be giving his tribute to Tara in a few minutes in the dining room. Please feel free to join us," Cybil said.

"Thank you." Faith made her way to the dining room, wondering what Pierce might have to say about Tara. He claimed to scarcely know her, so it seemed odd that he'd volunteer to pay her tribute.

The dining room was filling up fast, and Faith took a seat at a table.

Cybil stepped up to the podium. "Good morning, everyone. I wanted to start off by apologizing for disturbing your sleep last night. I hope the good-luck charms and pleasant music start today off right, even if you're still feeling a little sleep-deprived." She paused. "Of course, the pranks were meant to be a taste of what you put your readers through, which does include keeping them up at night." She grinned. "At least we hope we do, right?"

The group broke into applause.

"Now sadly, we lost a promising young writer far too young. Tara Blue was a journalist as well as an aspiring horror novelist. Many of you will remember her by her bubbly personality and beautiful smile. We are honored to have her mother visiting with us for the remainder of the weekend." Cybil gazed down at the podium for a moment. "While her passing was meant to be an act, as many of you assumed at first, I'm sorry to say it was all too real. And I'm sure we'll feel her loss for a long time to come."

Several women dug tissues out of their purses.

"Pierce Baltimore has volunteered to present a memorial tribute to Tara this morning," Cybil continued, "by reading one of her unpublished short stories." She left the podium and sat down at a nearby table.

Pierce took Cybil's place at the podium. Over the days of the retreat so far, he'd worn finely tailored and crisply starched dress shirts and pants, but this morning, he'd added a conservative striped tie and suit jacket to the ensemble. If he hadn't had a permanent grimace, he actually would have been quite handsome. Pierce set a piece of paper on the podium and adjusted the mic, appearing nervous.

He cleared his throat. "Tara's mother, Ruth, selected this short story for us to hear from among several Tara had written, and I think it is an excellent example of the tremendous promise her storytelling showed." He looked down at the paper and cleared his throat a second time, then announced the title of the story.

Pierce had a great voice, and he knew just how to build the tension and suspense with his pacing and tone.

Everyone jumped at several places in the story while Tara's mom simply smiled, her eyes watery.

Faith studied the guests as she listened. Some people like Eudora, the sweet, gray-haired woman Faith had sat beside at lunch earlier in the week, watched Pierce as he read. A few stared at the floor or at their table. Others simply sat with their eyes closed. If anyone was contemplating murderous thoughts against Pierce, Faith couldn't pick that person out.

She scanned the room again, this time concentrating on what guests were doing with their hands. Some fiddled with their breakfast spoons or napkins. Others drummed their fingers on the table. Two or three, including Nolan, clenched their fists. Cybil tapped on her phone, not seeming to listen at all.

Faith tamped down a burst of irritation at her rudeness. No one would believe her earlier words were genuine if they saw her now. Why couldn't she ignore her phone for five minutes to pay tribute to a fellow writer?

Cybil glanced up at Pierce. Then her gaze shifted and collided with Faith's. At least the woman had the decency to look ashamed. Cybil dropped her cell phone into her purse.

Pierce concluded the story to a standing ovation, and Cybil projected a picture of Tara on the wall behind the podium.

After the applause abated, Cybil thanked Pierce for the reading, extended her sympathies once more to Tara's mother, and then noted the highlights of the day's schedule.

Once people began filing out, Faith went up to Cybil. "That was beautifully done. I had no idea Pierce could read so well."

Cybil nodded. "I have to admit he did do a great job."

"I understand he volunteered to present the tribute," Faith said. From the argument she'd witnessed between Tara and Pierce, Faith thought he would be the least likely person to do that.

"Yes, and it surprised me," Cybil admitted. "He suggested it the second I got back from the yacht tour."

The yacht tour took place after Faith had caught Pierce going through Tara's things. So he'd made his lie as close to the truth as he could the instant he'd had the chance.

Faith watched Pierce return Tara's story to Ruth. From his tight expression, Faith sensed he hadn't gotten out of her what he'd hoped. And Faith suspected that whatever he'd wanted to get his hands on was still among Tara's belongings.

Was it something the note writer would have killed Tara to get back? Something Pierce might use to barter for his own life?

11

Faith asked Tara's mom if they might talk privately in the library. Faith needed to open it for guests, but based on the lack of traffic yesterday afternoon, she doubted they'd be disturbed.

Three steps into the library, Ruth turned all the way around, her gaze drifting to the open second story, circled by a balcony and filled with books, and finally to the extraordinary painted ceiling reminiscent of ancient chapels. "Wow, this is something." She ran her fingers along the intricate carvings decorating the walnut mantelpiece over the fireplace. "Tara must have loved this room."

Faith breathed in the comforting smell of beloved books. "It's a special place," she agreed.

"Tara loved to read anything she could get her hands on. She especially loved *Gulliver's Travels*." Ruth's voice hitched. "I can't tell you how many times she asked me to read it to her when she was a child. We had picture books and an easy reader version, but once she'd heard the entire novel, there was no going back."

"It's certainly a story that has captured imaginations for centuries." Faith grabbed a notepad and pen and then indicated the chairs at the table. "Let's have a seat, shall we?"

Ruth discreetly dabbed at her eyes with a tissue, then set her bag on the table and pulled out a stack of file folders and notepads. "These are all the notes Tara had with her. And I brought a couple of notepads from her desk at home. I was hoping we might find the name of the person who sent her that awful note."

Faith reached for the top file folder. "May I?"

"Of course. Two pairs of eyes are better than one."

Faith's neck prickled with the sensation there was another pair of eyes on them. She squinted up at the library's balcony, even though logically she knew she hadn't heard anyone come in. Then again, there were so many secret passageways in the manor . . .

Seeing no one, she returned her attention to the table. The first folder Faith opened contained what appeared to be research notes for an article or a novel. Some pages had lists of questions, and others had random observations or quotes. "How many of these papers did you allow Pierce to peruse?"

"None. I just gave him the story I thought he should read." Ruth stifled a shiver. "There was something about his eagerness that didn't feel right to me." She lowered her voice. "Besides, I knew Tara had done an article on him. I didn't want him finding her notes on it and maybe doing something with them before I had a chance to ensure everything was all right."

"I'm glad to hear it. I probably should have told you when you arrived that I found him in your daughter's room searching through her papers the morning after her death. He claimed he was looking for a piece for the tribute."

"He's an odd duck," Ruth said. "But lots of writers are. Too much time spent alone in their imaginary worlds, I think."

"I never thought of it that way."

"He received a threatening note, so at least now we know he didn't kill my Tara, right?" Ruth punctuated the conclusion by poking the file folder in front of her with her pen.

"I don't think we should take anything for granted."

Ruth's bottom lip trembled.

Faith's heart ached for her. "Are you sure you're okay with my going through these notes?"

Ruth blinked back tears. Apparently the strength she'd attempted to exude moments earlier was fading fast. "Yes, we need to do this." She opened one of the notepads to the first page. "Tara started this one when she arrived here. Take a look at these notations she made in the margins."

"It says 'Bill,' and next to his name she wrote 'MV,'" Faith said. "If

I were to hazard a guess, I'd say she was contemplating doing an article on the vet who is working with our concierge vet this week. His name is Bill, and he's from Martha's Vineyard."

"How did Tara know him?"

"She met him when he examined Midnight." Faith scanned the next few pages, but she didn't see any more notations. "Were there other notes?"

Ruth frowned at the book. "Yes, it was the very next page." She leafed back through them. "Maybe a couple of pages stuck together." She flipped the second page forward and back, frowning. "It's gone." She pointed to the small bits of paper still clinging to the metal spiral center. "Someone ripped it out."

Faith's heart thumped. Had Pierce snuck back in sometime after Ruth arrived and gone through the notebook? Or had someone else? "Do you remember what the notation said?"

"Yes, it simply said 'Carrie' with a question mark. And then 'Susan' with a question mark."

"Oh, I can explain that one," Faith said. "Tara thought she recognized our housekeeper Carrie from a past writers group meeting. But it seemed to be a case of mistaken identity. Perhaps Susan is the writer she mistook her for."

"Did Tara seem worried the young woman might be Susan?"

Faith mentally replayed what she could recollect of Tara's expression and tone when she'd asked about the housekeeper. "No, not that I perceived. She'd seemed disappointed and a tad confused when she found out Carrie wasn't who she'd thought."

Ruth tapped the notebook. "Something about this young woman must be significant."

"Honestly, it just seemed like a simple case of mistaken identity."

"Then why did someone go to the trouble of stealing the page?"

The question pulled Faith up short. "Do you remember what else was written on the front or back of it?"

Ruth closed her eyes as if visualizing the page. "It was full of questions. You know—the who, what, where kind. I can't remember any of them specifically, except the last one."

"What was that?"

"It said, 'What am I supposed to do?'"

They definitely needed to locate the missing page. Spotting Cybil passing by the library door, Faith asked Ruth to excuse her for a moment.

When Faith caught up to Cybil in the Great Hall Gallery, she said, "Do you know who Susan is? Her last name, I mean. She was a writer in your group."

Cybil shook her head. "I couldn't say. So many writers come and go. I think we've had a few Susans over the years."

"Only one memorable one, though," Eudora chimed in. She walked around the Agatha Christie statue and joined them. "Excuse me for sticking my nose into your conversation, but I couldn't help but overhear."

"No apology needed," Faith assured her. "What can you tell me about this memorable Susan?"

"Susan Moore was a student in Mr. Baltimore's writing workshops, and he became her mentor. Susan told me he'd led her to believe that her manuscript was almost ready for publication. Then because she'd burst into laughter at one of his book readings and thoroughly embarrassed him, he dropped her like a hot potato. Her outburst wasn't deliberate or even her fault. The poor young woman has IEED."

"What's that?" Faith asked.

"Involuntary emotional expression disorder. I think a childhood head trauma caused it. Susan said that her symptoms are fairly well controlled by medication, but every once in a while she's overcome by a sudden bizarre or inappropriate emotional reaction to something."

"I've never heard of the condition," Faith said.

"Neither had I before I met her."

Cybil snorted. "It seems psychologists have a disorder to explain away every manner of rude behavior these days."

Eudora gave Cybil a disapproving look. "The reactions are involuntary. Anyway, Mr. Baltimore didn't want anything more to do with her. He stopped taking her calls and even stopped attending our writers group meetings for a while. He didn't come back until Susan had left the group."

Faith thanked the two women for their help.

Brooke, who'd been putting the finishing touches on her refreshments and discreetly listening in, motioned Faith over. "It sounds like this Susan person has plenty of motive to target Pierce. Is she at the manor? How did you hear about her?"

"Based on a notation in Tara's notebook, we think Tara mistook Carrie for Susan."

"Our Carrie? In housekeeping?"

"Yes," Faith said. "Now that I think about it, I remember Tara mentioning Carrie looked like a writer she'd met at one of their meetings, but her name was different. Although I did notice her studying Carrie a couple of times after that, almost as if she couldn't believe Carrie wasn't who she thought."

Brooke frowned. "Aren't all these guests part of the same writers group?"

"I think so. Why?"

"If Carrie is this oh-so-memorable Susan person, how is it that only Tara recognized her?"

"Good point." Faith walked over to Eudora. "Excuse me. One more question. Did you happen to see Susan here this week?"

"No, dear. If she'd been here, we would have heard the fireworks the minute she ran into Mr. Baltimore."

Faith thanked her and rejoined Brooke. "I need to get back to the library. I left Ruth waiting in there."

"I'll come with you." Brooke scanned the hall, probably scouting for Marlene. "It's my break time anyway."

Faith and Brooke sat at the table with Ruth and filled her in on what they'd learned.

"Susan definitely sounds like someone with a motive to target Pierce," Brooke said.

Faith nodded. "I'm surprised he didn't mention her to the police. Although he's so self-centered, it probably never occurred to him that he'd treated the woman horribly."

Ruth planted her elbows on the table in front of her and dropped her head into her hands with a deep sigh. "But it doesn't explain Tara's death."

Faith winced. *Maybe she really did die of natural causes.*

Ruth sat up abruptly. "Unless Carrie *is* Susan! Maybe she's here to take revenge on Pierce. And when Tara recognized her, she got worried Tara would foil her plans."

Faith shook her head. "Most of the members of the writers group are here, including Pierce himself, and none of them have claimed that Carrie is Susan. Not to mention I can't imagine Carrie plotting anything sinister. She's afraid of her own shadow."

Ruth slumped in her chair once again.

Aunt Eileen, dressed in her gardening clothes—dirt-stained jeans and a flannel shirt—tapped on the terrace door.

Faith hurried over to let her in. "I didn't know you were working in the garden today." Her aunt and the other members of the garden club in town often volunteered to help with the extensive Victorian gardens, especially with projects that were too much for the Castleton staff.

Eileen stepped inside, and the scent of salt air drifted in with her. "I decided to help out at the last minute. There's always so much to do in the autumn before the snow starts falling. What are you working on?"

Faith introduced Eileen to Ruth. She invited her aunt to join them at the table, then updated her on what they knew.

Eileen glanced through Tara's files and notebooks. "Perhaps you're looking at this all wrong."

Ruth tilted her head. "How do you mean?"

"What if Pierce's note was a ruse?" Eileen asked. "After all, the killer got away with Tara's murder, so why attract police attention by openly threatening Pierce?"

"Maybe his compulsion to taunt Pierce overpowered his concern about getting caught," Brooke suggested.

"Wait," Faith said. "I think Aunt Eileen might be onto something here. What is the one thing the note achieved?"

"It made Pierce look innocent," Eileen said matter-of-factly.

"Exactly." Faith glanced around the otherwise-empty library to make sure no one was listening and lowered her voice. "So let's suppose he isn't. I saw him and Tara arguing the morning of her death. And from the way he was searching through her papers, I suspect that at the very least he was worried they might reveal something about him he didn't want exposed."

"So by writing the note," Eileen continued, "Pierce took any potential heat off himself."

"But if all that is true," Brooke said, "he wouldn't want to risk the police scrutinizing Tara's death more closely either."

"And he wouldn't have been the one who sent Tara the letter accusing her of whitewashing scum," Ruth pointed out.

"Although," Brooke mused, "if Pierce has that big of a secret, maybe he's the scum Tara supposedly whitewashed. I mean, I know we went through Tara's notes for the interview last night and she reported verbatim what was in them, but what if Pierce said a few things off the record?"

"Or perhaps she stumbled onto his secret later?" Eileen suggested.

Brooke fluttered her hands as if an even better idea had occurred to her and she couldn't spit it out fast enough. "If she was being pressured by someone else to expose the truth, it would have worried Pierce. And given him a motive."

A loud *whack* sounded from the direction of the stacks, followed by the first few notes of the theme music from *Psycho*.

The women spun around as one.

"What was that?" Brooke blurted.

"Hello? Is someone there?" Faith called out, glancing down the nearest aisle.

A shadow behind the bookcase darted away, leaving a book lying open facedown on the floor.

12

Faith rescued the fallen book as Brooke dashed up the next aisle.

A moment later Brooke escorted Carrie back to the group.

"I'm sorry," Carrie said. "I swear I wasn't doing anything wrong. Someone left that book on a table in the den, and I was just returning it. Then my phone went off, and I accidentally shoved the book straight through and off the other side when I jumped to silence it."

"Why didn't you bring it straight to me in the first place? Why skulk about the stacks?" Faith examined the spine of the fallen book, then smoothed the crumpled pages and carefully closed it.

"I saw you all talking and didn't want to disturb you." Carrie ducked her head. "I figured I could shelve it myself."

"The book fell before your phone went off. What really made you so jumpy?" Brooke prompted.

Carrie scuffed her foot against the floor. "I heard one of you say Pierce might have had a motive to kill that poor woman."

Faith scrutinized her, wondering if that was what had made her jumpy or if it had been overhearing her own name batted around. "We'd appreciate it if you didn't mention what you overheard to anyone."

"No, of course not." Carrie crossed her heart and then raised her hand as if making a vow.

Guests meandered in and eyed them curiously.

"You'd better get back to work," Faith said to Carrie. They didn't have time to question her further at the moment.

Faith showed a couple of browsing guests to the section of Gothic books they were curious about, then returned to the table.

"I'm afraid I can't stay any longer," Brooke said. "I need to get back to work or Marlene will be searching for me. But I'll give Midge a call.

I saw her SUV parked at the stables when I drove in this morning. She might have time to help."

"Who's Midge?" Ruth asked.

"The vet," Faith said. "She was here last night."

"Oh, I remember her now. I've met so many people. It's difficult to keep them all straight."

"We're all part of a book club at the Candle House Library in town," Eileen explained. "We enjoy a good mystery, although Brooke favors the romances. Anyway, our little group has managed to work out a few real-life mysteries. Haven't we, Faith?"

Faith nodded.

"Yes, Ms. Russell said as much about Faith," Ruth said, her expression hopeful. "Shall we continue?"

Eileen pulled a piece of paper out of her jacket pocket. "I've already jotted down some questions I had after reading the article Tara wrote about Pierce as well as her story about the mafia bribes. But with Pierce being here and maybe producing that note, I think we should go through the story Tara wrote about him more carefully."

"Okay, what's your first question?" Faith asked.

"Pierce talked extensively about his research trips," Eileen said. "It sounds as if getting the details right is very important to him. He always visits the locations where he sets his books and interviews the locals. So I was thinking. What if one of the people he talked to inadvertently shared information someone else didn't want getting out?"

"That's an interesting theory," Faith said.

"Or what if Pierce took some fascinating town tidbit or folklore and fictionalized it in a way that angered the real people involved?" Eileen continued.

"Oh yes," Ruth chimed in. "Authors used to tell Tara that they get letters from irate readers demanding to know why they used their spouse's name or their child's name for the villain in their novel. It's as if they're clueless that hundreds of people might share the name and the author likely had never met the person."

"Perhaps we should compile a list of the villains' names from Pierce's books to see if anything pops out," Faith said. "What else?"

"Pierce interviews a lot of experts, and he seeks hands-on experiences as much as possible." Eileen checked her notes. "For example, he went so far as to let someone use pepper spray on him so he could accurately write about how it felt."

"Really?" Faith responded. "Now that's dedication."

"Once Pierce torched an abandoned wooden boat to see how well it would burn, being waterlogged and all," Eileen went on. "What if an expert shared insider information with him, and he spun a story around it without giving any credit to his advisers?"

"Even more maddening than that is when someone finds out you're a writer," interjected a library browser with a book in hand, presumably to check out. "The first thing they want to do is tell you all about the story they plan to write someday."

The woman's friend nodded. "You can imagine that over the weeks and months afterward how little bits of that story might unintentionally filter into an author's work in progress without them ever remembering they'd heard it from someone else. But you can be sure that if the person recognizes his idea in an author's published story, he'll cry foul."

"Do you know if that's happened to any of the writers in your group?" Faith asked them.

"Sure. It happened to me," the second woman said. "But the accuser dropped the suit when he realized that I don't even make a livable paycheck from my writing."

"And his lawyer probably told him that his accusation would be difficult to prove, not to mention costly," her companion added.

"Have you ever heard of it happening to Pierce Baltimore?" Ruth asked.

Both women shook their heads.

"If it did happen, I doubt that he'd share it with us anyway," the second woman replied. "I imagine a best seller wouldn't want to give people ideas, especially if he quietly settled out of court."

"Or—"

Faith cut off Eileen's excited exclamation with a surreptitious glance and then thanked the women for their insights as she checked out their books.

After the women had meandered out of the library, Faith smiled at her aunt. "Sorry to cut you off, but I didn't want our theories spreading like wildfire among the guests. Who knows what the repercussions would be?"

Eileen splayed her hand over her neck as if contemplating the killer attempting to silence her. "Good thinking."

"What were you going to say?" Ruth asked.

"Oh, right. What if someone confronted Pierce like what happened to the woman who just left, maybe even filed a lawsuit?" Eileen said. "That might make him angry enough to take his revenge another way."

"It sounds like a possibility," Faith said. "But none of what we've come up with so far implicates Pierce. If there are any viable suspects, why wouldn't he be forthcoming to the police about them?"

"Well, he did say that lots of his fans have threatened him," Ruth reminded her. "But he'd never taken the threats seriously before."

"Perhaps he's been compiling a list we don't know about for the police," Eileen said. "Since the chief asked me to pull those articles, I could call him and casually share some of our theories to find out if Pierce has been more forthcoming since last night. If nothing else, it might give the police added incentive to dig deeper."

"That would be great," Ruth said.

A tap at the terrace window made them all jump.

Eileen darted a glance at the woman standing outside, holding a spade and wearing an amused expression. "Oh dear, I've neglected my gardening duties. I'd better get back outside. But don't worry. I'll make that call and let you know what Chief Garris says." She tucked her copy of Tara's article back into her pocket and hurried outside.

Faith picked up the pen and flipped to a blank piece of paper in her notepad. She wrote *Who, What, Where, When,* and *Why* across the top of the page. "Okay, so for who and why, we're thinking it could be Pierce because he feared Tara might expose some dark secret."

"Or it could be someone who is furious that Tara didn't report the truth about Pierce or someone else," Ruth said, "and he believes they both should be punished."

"Maybe it's someone who is angry with Pierce for some slight and came to exact his or her revenge, but Tara threatened to foil the plans." Faith glanced at her notes. "Anyone else?"

"I think that about covers it," Ruth said. "Susan fits into the last one, right?"

Faith mulled over Carrie's reaction to what she'd overheard. It seemed unlikely that Pierce wouldn't recognize her if she was Susan. And she did seem to be a nervous type in general. But what if there was more to it? Carrie had been helping Cybil a lot. Maybe even spying for her?

She tapped the pen to her lips. Cybil made no effort to hide how much she loathed Pierce, but did she loathe him enough to kill him? "We still don't have a clue what Pierce did that could drive someone to murder."

"Except for what he did to Susan," Ruth reminded her. "That writer told you Susan has a condition that could have caused her to act out irrationally. Perhaps she suddenly viewed Tara as a threat when she'd originally only intended to make Pierce pay."

Faith scrutinized what she'd written. "Except if Tara *was* murdered, the killer left no trace. That takes planning and skill. It doesn't fit with someone who is acting on impulse."

Ruth deflated. "You're right."

"We know the where and when for Tara's death," Faith went on, continuing to jot down notes. "And the note writer seems to want us to believe Pierce's death is imminent."

"It would help to know where Pierce has been recently that might have aggravated someone," Ruth said.

Faith made a note of that. "What's significant about when these threats happened?"

"They coincide with the horror retreat."

"They also coincide with the recent release of Pierce's new book," Faith stated. "What if something in the book set the note writer off?"

"We should find out where he researched it."

"Given how long it takes a book to go through a publisher's pipeline, that would have been over a year ago," Faith said.

"Sure, but maybe the note writer didn't know it would be in the book until the book came out. Do you think Pierce will tell us where he went?"

"If he won't, it pretty much reinforces our suspicion he has something to hide."

Ruth blew out a breath. "I think I'm starting to understand why the police seem so uncooperative. There are too many ifs and too few facts. We don't even know how Tara died."

"How," Faith repeated and added it to her page. "I forgot to include that question."

Midge strode into the library, smelling faintly of horse. "Did y'all hear the news?" Originally from Alabama, she sometimes still slipped into her distinctive Southern accent.

Ruth sprang to her feet, hope in her eyes. "What news?"

Midge's expression sobered, as if suddenly uncertain how Ruth would take the announcement. She lowered her voice. "Chief Garris says the coroner found a puncture mark on Tara's body."

Tears filled Ruth's eyes. "So . . ." She faltered over whatever she'd been about to say. She swallowed hard, then tried again. "They're finally going to try to find the person who killed my baby?" she said breathlessly.

Midge gave Ruth a kind smile. "Yes."

Ruth burst into tears.

Faith's heart went out to Ruth, and she wrapped her arms around the older woman.

After a moment Ruth stepped out of Faith's embrace and swiped at her damp cheeks. The woman was still clearly in shock despite the fact that the news confirmed what she'd suspected all along.

"Can I get you a glass of water or a cup of tea?" Faith asked.

Ruth dropped back into her seat. "No, I'm okay. Did the chief say anything else?"

"I didn't talk to him myself," Midge admitted. "Brooke called me to see if I had time to drop in and help with your research. I was heading here when Marlene asked me to take an inventory of all the veterinary drugs on the grounds—at the kennels, the stables, and the pet spa."

Faith gasped. "The police think a veterinary drug was used to kill Tara?"

"They didn't say. They only asked Marlene for a list of drugs on the premises. They probably want to see which ones they need to add to the next tox screen. Anyway, Marlene wants the list immediately, so I'm afraid I can't sit in on your brainstorming session."

"That's okay. I'm ready for a break anyway." Ruth gave Faith an apologetic look. "I'm sure you have other work you need to do too. Now that I know the police are taking this investigation seriously, my anxiety should ease a little." She gathered the files and notepads from the table and slipped them into her bag. "I think I'll take a walk outside."

"You do that," Faith urged. "We'll keep you posted if we learn anything new."

Ruth nodded and walked out the door.

"I'll give you a hand," Faith said to Midge. She motioned to the empty room. "I suspect Cybil has all the guests busy in workshops at the moment."

She accompanied Midge to the pet spa, where there was a small fridge and a cupboard with several mild medicines for small pets.

Midge wrote down the name of each item, along with its quantity, on a clipboard. "There's nothing missing from here. Let's check the stables next. It would have been easy for someone to find plenty of sedatives or painkillers in there."

Outside, the sound of a chain saw instantly sent Faith's thoughts to images of horror flicks. "What is that?"

"One of the groundskeepers is clearing away the debris from the tree that was struck by lightning," Midge said.

They waved to Ruth, who'd joined Eileen and two other volunteers in the Victorian garden trimming back dying flowers. A few weeks ago the garden had still been full of fragrant, colorful flowers. But now the drooping, decaying blossoms made a gloomy backdrop to Ruth's immense loss. Faith's heart stuttered at the thought.

They passed the topiaries before tramping down the hill to the stables.

"Bill didn't come in with you today?" Faith asked.

"He did. After Brooke called, I got permission for him to take a horse out for a ride."

The sound of galloping hooves approached.

"There he is now," Midge said. "He must have seen us coming."

Bill reined in the horse as he reached their side. "Is break time over already?"

"I'm afraid so," Midge replied. "I need to take a drug inventory for the assistant manager. But Faith's giving me a hand so you don't have to stop riding yet."

"That's okay," Bill said. "My sore rump is reminding me how out of practice I am. I'll rub the horse down and then be right in to help."

"It looks as if you've been working him too hard," Faith teased when they entered the stable and Bill was out of earshot. "It doesn't seem like he's had time to shave since he's been here."

"He told me he forgot to pack his razor and decided to try and grow a beard," Midge said distractedly.

The dusty air in the small office space at the end of the windowless tack room was as oppressive as the thoughts Faith suspected were weighing on Midge's mind.

Midge silently noted each drug and its quantity. She frowned as she compared the list to her treatment notes and previous inventory list.

"Is something missing?" Faith asked, unable to bear the silence any longer.

The soft nicker of a horse drifting into the room seemed to shake a little of the melancholy from Midge's mood. "No, everything seems to be accounted for. I just need to check the office at the kennels."

Bill joined them as they opened the kennel office. "I thought I'd take care of inventorying these for you." He went over to the fridge and removed the vials. He turned too quickly, and the vials caught the edge of the fridge door and shattered on the cement floor. Bill groaned. "So much for trying to help. I'm sorry."

"No problem." Midge poised her pen over her clipboard. "What was in the vials? I'll record them as destroyed."

"Sux," Bill said, shutting the fridge door. "I'll get something to clean up the mess." He grabbed a broom and a dustpan and started sweeping.

"Succinylcholine. Now there's a near-perfect choice," Midge commented.

Bill stopped sweeping and gave her an odd look.

"Perfect choice for what?" Faith asked.

"To kill someone," Midge explained. "Think about it. Very little is required. It's easy to inject, and it paralyzes muscles, including those responsible for respiration, in under a minute. Also, it metabolizes quickly, making it virtually undetectable by the time a victim is found."

Faith's skin crawled. "If it's so lethal, then what do *you* use it for?"

"To relax patients before intubation," Bill said, sweeping the broken vials onto a dustpan.

"So a machine would need to be breathing for them?" Faith asked.

"Exactly," Midge said. "And the drug wears off within ten minutes or so, but if the patient isn't on a respirator, that's enough time to die from lack of oxygen."

"But the drug wouldn't show up in a tox screen?" Faith reiterated.

"It's unlikely because of how fast the body metabolizes it." Midge squatted in front of the short fridge and counted the vials inside.

Faith noted the names and amounts on Midge's clipboard.

After Midge had finished going through everything inside, she closed the fridge and took the clipboard to the desk where her treatment journal sat open. She glanced from one page to the other, checking things off, and furrowed her brow.

"What's wrong?" Faith asked.

"I'm not sure." Midge peered into the trash can where Bill had dumped the broken vials. "How many vials were you holding? Do you know?"

"A couple," Bill answered.

"Two exactly?" Midge persisted.

"Maybe three. Why?" Bill asked.

"I thought I saw two." Faith peeked at the remnants in the otherwise empty can. "Look. There are only two plastic caps."

Midge nodded, but her frown deepened.

"Some are missing," Faith guessed.

Midge nodded with a frustrated sigh. "Four vials, counting the two that just broke."

"Would two have been enough to . . . ?" Faith's heart cracked at the anguish in Midge's face.

"Yes, it would have been enough to kill Tara," Midge whispered. "I should have had the sux under lock and key." Her voice rose angrily. "What was I thinking? It was irresponsible."

"It isn't your fault," Faith said. "You keep the office locked."

"Sure, but the kennel staff are in and out of here all the time.

Any one of them could leave it unlocked. I should have had stricter safeguards in place. I wouldn't be surprised if Marlene fires me over this. The veterinarians' board might even revoke my license."

"Surely not. There's no way you could have predicted this," Faith said, trying to calm her friend.

Bill closed the office door. "Only Faith and I know what you discovered. And I won't say anything."

Faith gaped at him. She understood that he was trying to spare Midge from trouble, but if the police were to have any hope of finding Tara's murderer, they needed to know the drug that may have killed her could very well have come from this office.

Bill snatched a couple of stray vial caps from the shelf along the wall and tossed them into the trash can. "In fact, it looks to me like I'm to blame for all four of them."

Midge shook her head. "I appreciate that you want to protect me. But the police need to know what I've found."

He gave her a sad smile. "You're doing the right thing."

13

"The police are here," Faith announced from the window.

Midge sat in the kennel office, still poring over her treatment journal. "I was hoping I'd simply missed recording administering the succinylcholine. But no such luck." She closed the book with a frustrated sigh and pushed stiffly to her feet.

When Faith opened the side door to let in Officer Mick Tobin, she spotted Marlene stalking down the driveway toward them in a navy-blue dress and shiny gold heels. "Did you call Marlene?" Faith asked Midge. "She looks as if she's on a rampage."

"She's not going to be any happier when she gets here."

Tobin walked in and greeted them. Faith respected the officer. He was serious about his job, but he also had a good sense of humor.

Marlene strode inside and joined them.

Tobin opened his notepad and addressed Midge. "Why don't you tell me what you found?"

"The problem is what we *didn't* find." Midge explained what was missing and how it might have been used to kill Tara.

Marlene crossed her arms. Her face had grown redder as Midge recounted her discovery, and she seemed to be fighting the urge to add questions of her own. She clearly wasn't thrilled to be learning of the news at the same time as Tobin. Not that she would have been thrilled to learn it anytime. At least this way, she might cool down a bit before she had a chance to have a go at Midge.

"Who has access to this fridge?" the officer asked.

"I lock the office whenever I leave, but the kennel staff uses it too." Midge scrubbed her hand over her face, looking more ragged than Faith had ever seen her. Her trademark fuchsia lipstick was a ghost of its usual brightness. And her shoulder-length blonde hair was a rat's nest from the way she'd been plowing her fingers through it. "But more than once the office has been open when I've come in," Midge added.

Tobin scribbled in his notepad. "Who else has keys?"

"Besides the kennel staff, Mr. Jaxon and Ms. Russell," Midge answered.

"Does the cleaning staff have keys?" Tobin asked the assistant manager.

Marlene nodded.

Tobin studied Bill. "And who are you?"

"Dr. Stephenson." Bill shook Tobin's hand. "I'm a vet from Martha's Vineyard. Dr. Foster has been kind enough to let me tag along with her for a few days to see how her concierge service operates."

"So you had access?"

"Sure."

Midge glanced at Marlene, no doubt thinking this would be another strike against her.

"Several guests also visit their pets here daily," Bill pointed out. "Any one of them could have slipped into the office."

Tobin made note of the fact. "But the two of you had the easiest access and the most knowledge about what to do with the drugs, correct?"

"Neither of them even knew Tara beyond treating her cat for all of fifteen minutes," Faith protested.

"Can you provide me with a list of the guests with pets in the kennels?" Tobin asked.

Midge quickly wrote the names on a piece of paper.

Faith pointed to Pierce's name. "Pierce was an army medic before he became a writer. So he'd know how to administer a drug."

"And Faith saw him arguing with Tara the morning she died," Midge said.

"What was the argument about?" Tobin asked Faith.

"I couldn't hear exactly what they were saying. I tried asking

Pierce last night after he got that threatening note, but he said he couldn't remember."

"I'll question him." To Midge, Tobin added, "Let me know if you think of anything else."

"Most of the guests are in a group discussion at the moment," Marlene advised Tobin, her tone amazingly even. "I can help you locate the ones you wish to interview, and you may use my office."

Marlene's office was in the basement, and Faith suspected she'd like nothing better than to keep the officer hidden down there, so as few people as possible would see him.

"I'll talk to *you* later," Marlene said to Midge.

And even Faith flinched at her tone this time.

"What are you going to do now?" Faith asked Midge once Officer Tobin and Marlene were gone.

She glanced at the treatment journal still sitting on her desk, opened to the current date, and sighed. "I think Bill and I should stick around in case Officer Tobin has more questions for us after speaking to the guests."

"We could pick up some locks," Bill suggested, "and get started on securing the remaining medicine. You know, to demonstrate that you're being proactive about ensuring nothing like this can happen again."

"That's a good idea," Faith said. She hoped keeping busy would take Midge's mind off the situation. "Meanwhile I'll walk back up to the manor and see if I can find out what Officer Tobin learns from our guests."

Midge didn't say anything as she closed the journal.

Faith knew her friend was worried that she somehow shared the blame in what had happened to Tara. She laid a hand on Midge's arm. "Even if your drugs were used, you're not responsible for someone else's horrible actions. Whoever it was would have found a way to kill Tara one way or the other, okay?"

Midge nodded.

A breathless Ruth intercepted Faith before she reached the manor. "I just saw Ms. Russell with a police officer, but I couldn't catch up to them before they hurried inside. Do you know why he's here? Do the police have a lead on Tara's killer?"

Grateful Ruth hadn't noticed that the officer had been at the kennels too—and reluctant to open Midge up to allegations when they didn't even know for sure if the missing sux had been used to murder Tara—Faith responded vaguely. "I will let you know as soon as I hear anything definitive," she assured the woman, then urged her to continue her walk in the gardens.

When Faith went inside, it was evident Marlene's hope to keep the police interviews discreet had been a pipe dream. The guests and more than a few staff members were gathered in the gallery, where Pierce stood toe to toe with Tobin.

Spotting Brooke on the sidelines, Faith quickly sidled over to her. "What happened?" she whispered.

"The group was heading for lunch when Officer Tobin asked Pierce if he could talk to him in Marlene's office. Pierce obviously assumed Officer Tobin was here about the note. Maybe he thought the police had ID'd fingerprints from it. So Pierce insisted there was no need to go to the office."

"Oh no," Faith said.

Brooke nodded. "The second Tobin asked Pierce if he'd gone into the vet's office for anything while at the kennels, Pierce blew his top. He demanded to know what that had to do with the threat against him."

Faith turned back to the conversation between Tobin and Pierce.

Stone-faced, Officer Tobin merely said, "If you'll come with me, we can clear this up in private."

"Clear what up?" Pierce demanded.

"The vet would keep meds in her office," one guest said to another. "Maybe some are missing. Something that could be lethal."

Pierce shot the person a scowl, then glared at Tobin. "Is that what this is about? Why are you asking me if I was in there? I'm the one being threatened."

"Could we go to Ms. Russell's office to discuss it?" the officer asked.

Pierce glared. "There's nothing to discuss. I go to the kennels every morning and afternoon to take my dog, Hannibal, for a walk. That's it. I have never even been near the vet's office. Ever."

"Let's talk about this in the office," Tobin insisted.

"You should be questioning the vet or the kennel staff. They have easy access." Pierce motioned to the staff loitering on the fringes of the room. "Or any of the staff likely has keys. The housekeepers have access to all the rooms, right?" He gestured at Carrie, then did a double take and blanched.

She smiled and walked away.

"Did you see that?" Faith said to Brooke.

"Yeah, it was as if he'd seen a ghost."

Officer Tobin and Marlene whispered to each other.

Marlene clapped. "Okay, everyone, the show's over. Your lunch is waiting for you." She glanced to Brooke for confirmation.

Brooke nodded and led the way to the dining room.

Marlene quietly snagged a guest at the back of the group, presumably another with a pet in the kennels, and headed downstairs with her.

Officer Tobin said to Pierce, "I might have more questions for you later. Stick around."

Faith intercepted Pierce before he could catch up to the departing group. "I couldn't help but notice that you seemed disturbed when you glanced at Carrie. Did you recognize her from somewhere?"

Pierce stood at least half a foot taller than Faith and looked down at her without bothering to mask his obvious irritation at being put on the spot yet again. "Who's Carrie?" he said, stuffing his hand into his sweater pocket.

"The housekeeper who was standing over there a few moments ago." Faith motioned to the spot.

Pierce waved his hand dismissively. "I don't know her. My mind must have been elsewhere. Excuse me." He bowed slightly, then strode off.

Faith glanced down where he'd been standing. Bits of paper littered the floor—the kind of paper bits that come off a page ripped from a spiral notebook.

Her gaze shot to the sweater pocket Pierce had pulled his hand from a moment earlier, and she hurried after him. "Excuse me."

He kept walking.

She reached forward and tapped his arm. "Mr. Baltimore, I'm sorry to bother you. Just one more question."

He spun on his heel and stared at her.

For a full five seconds Faith stood mute as she wondered how to get him to show her the paper.

Pierce raised his eyebrows. "Yes?"

"The paper in your pocket," she blurted out. "May I see it?"

He furrowed his brow. "What paper?" He thrust his hands into his pockets and held out their contents—a lozenge, a tissue, and a folded notebook page.

Resisting the urge to snatch it up, Faith gingerly pointed to the paper. "That one."

"Why do you want to see my brainstorming notes?" Pierce asked irritably, unfolding the page.

It was filled with who, what, where, and why questions, just as Ruth had described the page missing from Tara's notebook.

"Don't you mean Tara's notes? I believe Officer Tobin will be interested to know why you have a page torn from a murder victim's notebook in your pocket."

Pierce stared at her as if she had two heads and then chuckled. "I remember you. You're the one who found me going through Tara's notes."

Faith unconsciously rubbed her shoulder that had taken the brunt of the bookcase mishap. "And who spared you from getting hit by the fallen bookcase." Not to mention questioned him the night before about his argument with Tara. Carrie wasn't kidding when she said people never noticed the help.

"Ah." He had the good manners to appear contrite. "That was you? I don't think I ever properly thanked you."

Faith waited for him to do so now.

He didn't.

But Pierce did hand over the paper. "Feel free to show it to the officer. And if he'd like to compare the handwriting to my other notes, tell him he's welcome to come to my room to see them. I have nothing to hide. Except I don't normally allow others to read my working plot notes."

Faith frowned at the page. Had she been wrong? Or was that simply what he wanted her to believe?

Ruth and Nolan walked into the lobby. From the snatches of dialogue Faith caught, it sounded as if Nolan was reminiscing about a day he'd spent with Tara at a book festival.

"Ruth, could you please come here for a minute?" Faith asked.

She glanced curiously from Faith to Pierce before joining them, Nolan still at her side.

Faith showed her the notepaper. "Is this the missing page from Tara's notebook?"

Ruth eagerly reached for the paper but immediately shook her head. She flipped it over and glanced at the reverse side—something Faith should have done to see if the questions about Carrie that Ruth had mentioned were there. "No, this isn't Tara's handwriting."

"It's Pierce's," Nolan said. "I should know. He sent his first manuscript to me in that scrawl. I told him if he wanted me to be his agent, he needed to learn to type or hire a typist."

Pierce smirked. "I still write longhand, but at least I can afford the typist now."

"I'm terribly sorry." Faith returned the paper to him.

"No harm done," Pierce said magnanimously. "Perhaps you should try your hand at novel writing. You seem to have the imagination for it." He shifted his smirk to her as he stuffed the paper back into his pocket, then strode off.

"What was that about?" Nolan asked.

Ruth explained about the missing page from Tara's notebook.

Faith bristled, still not certain the former boyfriend could be trusted.

To Faith, Ruth said, "We heard a veterinary drug might have been used on Tara. Is that true?"

"Some stock of a drug is missing," Faith replied, "and the coroner will test Tara's blood for it. But I'm afraid it might be impossible to know for sure, because the body metabolizes the drug so quickly. It's unlikely the test would be positive even if the drug was the poison used."

"Don't you have security cameras? Or what about your cameraman?" Ruth motioned to the bulletin board next to them at the base of the staircase. It displayed an array of instant photos. "Maybe he caught the perpetrator sneaking into the vet's office."

Nolan scanned the photos. "All of these were taken in and around the manor or on the yacht." He sighed. "Even if we had a picture of someone going into the kennels, if the blood test comes back negative, the police would need a lot more corroborating evidence to make a case against someone."

Ruth squinted at the photos and pulled two from the board. "Look at this." She held one up. "Is that Pierce coming from the kennels?"

"But we already know he goes there twice a day to walk his dog," Nolan said.

"What about her?" Ruth pointed to a woman in the second picture, also appearing to be returning from the direction of the kennels or stables. "You're not going to tell me she was walking a dog in a dress."

"May I?" Faith took the snapshot and squinted at the tiny figure. The woman was wearing a lime-green dress.

It was the same dress Cybil had worn on the night Tara died.

14

The look Nolan exchanged with Faith suggested he also recognized Cybil's dress, but thankfully he didn't seem any more eager than Faith to speculate in front of Ruth. After all, even if it was Cybil in the photo, it didn't prove she'd stolen the drug.

"I'll see if I can get the digital files from the photographer so we can figure out who this might be," Faith offered. "In the meantime, why don't the two of you join the others for lunch?"

Nolan held out his arm for Ruth, and they headed to the dining room together.

Faith took the photo to the front desk and asked the clerk, "Do you know if the photographer who snapped these instant photos would also have a digital copy?"

"I bet he does. Some of the new instant cameras come with an SD card," Cara responded. "If you want to ask him yourself, I just saw him head into the dining room. His name is Jonathan Newell, and he's always carrying a camera."

"Thank you," Faith said, then slipped into the dining room to the hum of conversations and clatter of utensils on dishes. The delicious aroma of lamb stew made her stomach grumble.

She didn't see a guy with a camera or Cybil for that matter. Spotting Carrie leaving the room with a cart of empty serving dishes, Faith followed her. "Do you know where Jonathan, the group's photographer, went?"

Carrie paused in front of the elevator and hit the call button. "Ms. Russell fetched him to talk to Officer Tobin."

Faith nodded, then turned to see Ruth hurrying toward them.

The elevator door clunked open, and Carrie pushed the cart in.

"Susan!" Ruth called out, waving. She ran toward them.

Carrie pressed a button on the control panel without glancing at Ruth, and the doors closed.

Ruth skidded to a stop next to Faith, her face flushed. "Did she react at all to hearing the name Susan?"

"Not that I could tell," Faith said.

Ruth harrumphed. "Since we tend to respond automatically when we hear our name, I thought I might catch her unaware. I know the others all said Susan isn't here, but Tara was so good with faces."

Faith bit down on her bottom lip, a new concern gripping her. If Carrie *was* Susan in disguise, she now knew Ruth suspected as much. And if she was responsible for Tara's death, what might she do to Ruth?

"Why did you follow her?" Ruth asked.

"To ask her if she'd seen where the photographer went."

Ruth sighed. "Oh."

"Why don't you go back and finish your lunch?" Faith suggested. "You need to keep your strength up."

Ruth put a hand to her forehead. "No, I think I'll lie down for a while in my room. I'm afraid I feel a migraine coming on."

"I'm so sorry." Faith clasped her by the elbow and steered her to the elevator, then pushed the call button for her. "Can I get you anything for the pain?"

"No, I have medicine in my room. But please let me know if you hear of any new developments."

"I will. You get some rest now."

Ruth pushed the elevator button again and waited for its return.

Faith took the stairs to the basement in search of the photographer and found a man with a camera slung over his shoulder wandering the hallway. "Can I help you find something?" she asked.

"Yeah, I'm looking for the dining room. Don't want to miss lunch." He patted his stomach and grinned.

"It's upstairs on the first floor. By the way, I'm Faith, Castleton's librarian. You're Jonathan, the horror group's photographer, right?"

He nodded and lifted his camera. "I guess this gives me away."

"Yes, a little." She smiled. "I was wondering if I could get digital copies of the pictures you've taken so far."

"Do you want to immortalize us in the library archives?" Jonathan chuckled. He opened a little door on his camera and popped out the SD card. "Do you have a laptop handy?"

"Yes, in the library."

He handed her the SD card. "Feel free to pull the pictures from this. I'll stop by after lunch to pick it up."

"That's great. Thank you." Faith directed Jonathan upstairs to the dining room.

Ignoring her own growling stomach, she returned to the library. Her pulse jumped when she inserted her key into the door and realized it was already unlocked. She mentally replayed her earlier exit. *I locked it. I'm sure I did.*

Watson appeared out of thin air and rubbed against her legs.

She scooped him up. "Hey, Rumpy, did you come to be my bodyguard?" She held him tucked against her chest with one arm and slowly pushed open the door. "Hello," she called out cheerily. "Anybody in here?"

Her cell phone rang, making her jump.

Watson leaped from her arms and raced up the library stairs.

As Faith peered at the upper level from her spot near the door, she felt around in her purse for her phone. Answering it, she relaxed at the soothing sound of Wolfe's deep voice.

"The chief called to update me on the latest. Did you hear?"

"You mean that it looks as if Tara might have been poisoned?"

A rustling sound trickled down from the second level, and she stepped farther into the room to search for its source. "Could you please hold on a second?"

Faith headed up the stairs, scanning what she could see of the second level as she climbed. "Who's here?"

Watson trotted out from the stacks, appearing unconcerned by whatever he had or hadn't found.

Faith tilted her head and listened for sounds of anyone else up there with them. "Was it you making the rustling sound?" From her new vantage point at the railing on the second level, she gazed down at the main floor. "I probably just forgot to lock the door," she said to Watson. "This retreat has me so on edge."

Then she apologized to Wolfe for keeping him waiting. "I wanted to make sure there was no one around listening in," she explained and filled him in on the missing drugs from Midge's inventory.

"I should have installed security cameras in the stables and kennels," Wolfe said.

"I borrowed the images from the group's photographer. I'm going to download them to see if they might offer any clues."

"That's a good idea. I have a conference call in a few minutes, so I'll check in with you later. Please tell Midge not to blame herself."

Faith smiled. "Already done. But I know she'd be glad to hear it from you too."

"Then I'll be sure to tell her. I'll see you soon," Wolfe said. "In the meantime, be careful," he added sternly.

She chuckled. "Always." She clicked off the phone and headed to her desk to download the images before Jonathan arrived.

Faith copied the images to her laptop, but before she could study them, a few guests came in with questions and books to check in. She ejected the SD card and slid it into an envelope with the photographer's name on it, then closed her laptop and gave her full attention to the guests.

One aspiring author inquired about Castleton's history. "The manor would be a wonderful setting for a Gothic novel," she mused.

"I agree," Faith told her. "Our French Renaissance château-style mansion was built by a wealthy steamship merchant in 1895. The man endeavored to replicate the splendor of many of the architectural styles he'd seen abroad. For instance, the Paris Opera and other French buildings inspired the impressive music room."

"It sounds amazing. I'll have to check it out later," the writer said, then started browsing the shelves.

Faith returned to her desk, where Jonathan was waiting to pick up his SD card. She handed him the envelope with her thanks.

"The next workshop is about to start," he announced to the other guests availing themselves of the library.

Faith soon found herself alone once more. She returned the books to their shelves, then startled at the sight of two figures darkening the terrace door.

Aunt Eileen and Midge cupped their hands around their eyes and peered through the glass.

Faith opened the door for them. "What are you two doing? Why didn't you just come in?"

"We were checking to make sure there weren't a lot of guests in here first," Eileen said.

"Is Officer Tobin gone?" Faith asked.

Eileen nodded.

"Did he say anything else to you before he left?" Faith asked Midge.

"He dusted the fridge and cupboards for fingerprints and took mine and Bill's." She cringed.

Eileen put her arm around Midge's shoulder.

"But that was just to eliminate your fingerprints, wasn't it?" Faith said. "Because obviously yours and Bill's would be on the fridge and the medicine."

"You're right. But I'm more worried that they'll find my fingerprints on the smoking gun—or in this case the needle." Midge slumped into one of the armchairs near the fireplace. "If only I had kept everything locked up."

"It isn't your fault," Faith told her friend. "Wolfe feels the same way. He wanted me to tell you not to blame yourself."

Midge nodded, but she didn't appear convinced.

As Faith perched on a chair next to Midge, she thought of something. "Needles come in sterile packages, don't they?"

"Yes," Midge answered. "I keep my supply of sterile needles in the bag I carry around with me. But the killer wouldn't have cared whether the needle was sterile or not, so he could have easily fished one out of the sharps disposal container."

"Nolan is diabetic, so he probably has a container for his insulin needles," Faith said brightly, because the more suspects with easy access to needles, the lower the chances this would implicate her friend. "I wonder if Tobin knows about Nolan's diabetes."

"We'd better find out." Midge pulled her cell phone from her pocket. "Tobin took my sharps container to have the needles inside tested and dusted for fingerprints. If there are others on the premises, he'll want to know."

"Do you think a murderer would be stupid enough to dispose of the weapon in his own needle container?" Eileen asked. "He had to know it would have Tara's DNA on it."

"Maybe he didn't worry about it because he assumed it would look like she died from natural causes," Faith said.

Eileen perused the display of books by the visiting authors, lifted one from the shelf, and scanned the back cover. "As a literary agent, Nolan has probably read dozens of books in which the villain used sux as his weapon of choice. But why would he go to that much trouble and risk being caught when his own supply of insulin would have worked just as well?"

Faith's heart dipped at Eileen's question. It was a good one, and she couldn't begin to speculate on an answer. "We don't know for sure that sux was actually used to kill Tara, but it sure seems too coincidental that it should go missing the same week she dies."

Midge clicked off her phone and returned it to her pocket. "Officer Tobin is going to come back to talk to Nolan. He wasn't on the list of guests who'd been to the kennels, so he hadn't been on his radar earlier."

"Where's Bill?" Faith asked her.

Midge rose and began to pace. "I told him he could call it a day as soon as Tobin was done with us, since he had a dinner date with a woman he met at the coffee shop."

"What do you know about Bill?" Faith asked. "I mean, he kind of called you out of the blue about shadowing you this week, didn't he?"

Midge stopped pacing and stared at Faith, her eyes widening. "Do you think he has something to do with all this?"

Eileen put down the book she held and looked at Faith expectantly.

"I don't know," Faith said. "I can't imagine why. They didn't seem to know each other."

"But he had access to the drugs," Eileen reminded them.

Midge frowned.

"Like I said," Faith told her, "remember that we don't even know for sure it was sux that killed Tara."

"My friend Beth is a vet on Martha's Vineyard. She vouched for Bill," Midge said, returning to the chair she'd been sitting in. "Beth told me he was really nice and that she'd never heard any complaints about him professionally." She drummed her fingers on the armrest. "She hadn't heard about his concierge plan, though."

"Perhaps he wanted to keep it quiet," Eileen said. "He could have been worried about giving his competition ideas."

"That's what I'd thought too. But I should have asked more questions." Midge dug her phone out of her pocket and scrolled through the contact list. "Well, there's no time like the present." She tapped Beth's name to make the call.

"Ask her if Bill knows Pierce Baltimore," Faith said, thinking of the threatening note.

Midge nodded to Faith as she brought the phone to her ear.

Faith and Eileen listened to Midge's side of the conversation until she disconnected a few minutes later.

"Did she confirm that Bill knows Pierce?" Faith asked. After all, Martha's Vineyard was a popular destination for the rich and famous.

"Beth didn't have much to add to what she'd already told me before. She didn't think Bill knew Pierce personally, but she did remember him asking her if she'd ever read any of his novels. Apparently, he's been on a reading marathon of them for the past few months."

"Really? Don't you think it's strange Bill didn't mention that to you with Pierce Baltimore staying here this week?" Eileen asked. "For all we know, Bill concocted the concierge story just to have behind-the-scenes access to the man."

"I really believe he's sincere about wanting to become a concierge vet," Midge replied. "But I imagine if he'd heard Pierce was coming here, he'd try to coordinate his visit to coincide with Pierce's."

"He hardly had to do that when there's a public book signing tomorrow afternoon," Eileen pointed out.

"That's true. But this way he kills two birds with one stone and doesn't have to wait in line Sunday afternoon to talk to Pierce," Midge reasoned.

A chill ran up Faith's spine at the possibility that Pierce's note writer might have other plans for the book signing tomorrow afternoon.

15

As Midge and Eileen rose to leave the library, Faith said, "I was about to review the retreat photos on my laptop. Do you want to help?"

"Count me in," Eileen said.

"Me too." Midge dragged two extra chairs to Faith's desk. "Where did you get the photos?"

"I borrowed the photographer's SD card." Faith sat between Midge and Eileen and opened the file of photos. "Nolan, Ruth, and I saw a picture on the bulletin board that had a woman in a lime-green dress coming from the direction of the kennels in the background. I believe it was Cybil, and I'm hoping I can zoom in on her."

"Should we look for anything else?" Eileen asked.

"I also wanted to go through each picture on the screen where we can better see what the photographer incidentally captured in the background," Faith answered. "Maybe someone else will strike us as suspicious."

The initial few pictures showed guests posing in front of decorations in the gallery on the first day of the retreat.

"Look at the face on Cybil there," Eileen said right before Faith advanced to the next image.

Faith went back to the image. A pair of ladies chatted with Pierce, who appeared to be autographing a book for one of them. Cybil stood in the background, observing the exchange with a sour expression.

"Well, we already know there's no love lost between her and Pierce," Midge said. "The question is, does she despise him enough to kill him? And why would she target Tara?"

Faith clicked to the next photo. "That's assuming Pierce's note writer is the same person who killed Tara, not just someone who used her death as an opportunity to torment him."

"Yes, that sounds like something a rival like Cybil might do," Midge agreed.

"We know it is," Faith stated. "Because Cybil already admitted to writing a note like that. Carrie was supposed to deliver it to Pierce's room, but she never did."

"If I were Pierce's former agent, I might be tempted to torment him a little," Eileen ventured, then ducked her head as if embarrassed to admit as much.

Faith chuckled. "Wolfe asked Nolan outright if he wrote the note, and he denied it. But based on how he tried to shift attention to Cybil—"

"And the fact he knows his way around a needle," Eileen added.

"Yes. It does make me wonder if we can believe him." Faith went to the next image. She hadn't seen this one on display in the manor.

"Hey, that's Tara and you," Midge blurted out.

And Cybil. By the lion topiary that was meant to appear to attack Tara. Faith zoomed in on the background. "There's a dark shadow behind those bushes." She pointed at the screen. "Maybe it was someone listening in on the plan."

"You're missing the obvious," Eileen said. "If the photographer was close enough to capture this picture, he would have overheard the plan."

"But what motive would he have to kill Tara?" Midge asked.

"I don't know," Eileen said. "But it might be worth looking into."

"I suppose he could have offered her photos to accompany one of her articles," Midge speculated. "And then he got angry if she rejected them."

"He'd have to have serious anger control issues if that drove him to murder," Faith said.

"Maybe it was the last straw in a whole line of rejections," Midge suggested.

"I'll see what I can find out about him," Eileen volunteered. "What's his name?"

"Jonathan Newell." Faith clicked to the next photo.

A dozen images later, the one with the woman in the lime-green dress appeared. Faith zoomed in on her. "I'm sure that's the dress Cybil wore the night Tara died." She printed it out so she'd have a hard copy to show Wolfe later.

"If Cybil planned to sneak down to the kennels to steal drugs, why wait until after she changed into a dress and heels?" Midge said.

"And she's not carrying a bag of any kind," Eileen commented. "So she wouldn't have had an easy way to conceal it."

Faith begrudgingly conceded they were probably right and continued scrolling through the pictures. One showed Pierce heading to the kennel—a trip they already knew he made at least twice a day. None showed Nolan anywhere. The images soon rolled past the night of Tara's death.

"The rest of these aren't going to help us." Faith started to close the last photo.

"Wait. Look in the background." Midge pointed to the screen. "Cybil and one of the manor staff seem to be having quite an intense discussion."

"That's Carrie," Faith said. "She's been helping Cybil pull off her pranks. And I believe Marlene has given her approval."

Midge sighed. "Okay, so this was a bust."

"No, I'll check into the photographer's background," Eileen said. "It might turn up a new lead."

"I wish we could find that missing page from Tara's notebook," Midge remarked. "It must have something incriminating on it."

Faith filled them in on her embarrassing faux pas with Pierce when she'd thought he had the missing page. And it suddenly occurred to her that if Nolan had palmed the page, he now knew they knew it was missing and were trying to find it.

"I suppose if we were really ambitious," Midge said, "we'd dig through all the garbage bags for it."

Faith cringed at the thought.

"My sentiments exactly." Midge glanced at her watch. "I'd better go. I promised Peter I wouldn't work late today, and I still need to stop by the bakery."

"I'll walk out with you," Eileen said, then gave Faith a warm hug. "I'll call you later. Be careful. You never know who might be watching you."

"I will." Faith glanced up at the second-story balcony where she'd thought she'd heard someone when she first came in.

Midge and Eileen left by the terrace door, and Faith locked it behind them.

Watson scampered down the stairs from the second level.

Faith picked him up. "Were you keeping a lookout from up there? I think we're going to call it a day and go home. The retreat guests don't seem to be interested in browsing the library."

Watson meowed.

She laughed. "I thought you might be happy about that. But before we do, let's meander past the guest rooms."

Faith knew it was a long shot, but she figured if Nolan had snatched the page from Tara's notebook and hadn't gotten rid of it before the episode with Pierce, he might have since. And he wouldn't have been stupid enough to dispose of it in the trash can in his own room and risk incriminating himself if it was discovered.

Then again, if the page had incriminating information on it, he was more likely to shred or burn it. Or maybe flush it down the toilet.

Faith and Watson headed up the stairs. But before they'd even reached the second floor, where the guest rooms were located, Faith heaved a defeated sigh at the hopelessness of her idea. Exactly what was she expecting to find?

Carrie was vacuuming the hallway. Faith watched the dust swirl in the clear canister, and the sight of confetti-like bits of white paper caught her eye.

Faith signaled to Carrie to turn off the machine, then examined the contents of the canister. "Did you happen to notice where you picked up the paper bits?"

Carrie frowned. "Not a clue. Sorry."

Faith's heart kicked into a staccato rhythm. "No problem. Thanks." She considered how easily Carrie could have slipped into Tara's—now Ruth's—room and examined the notebooks undetected. If Carrie was somehow connected to all of this, she knew Ruth suspected her of being Susan. And she also had to realize Faith knew about the missing notebook page on which Tara had mused about Carrie and Susan being one and the same.

As the sound of Carrie's vacuum moved farther down the hall, Faith slipped into the housekeeper's closet where the cleaning carts were stored. She sifted through the clear garbage bags hanging on the carts, but there was no sign of a crumpled notebook page.

Carrie opened the closet and squealed when she saw Faith inside. "Is there a problem?"

"Uh, yes. One of the guests misplaced an important page from her notebook and is very distressed about it." Faith attempted to stick as close to the truth as possible in the hope that Carrie might have seen the page and not been the one to take it.

"Oh no! A manuscript page?"

"Brainstorming notes, I believe."

"That would be awful for a writer to lose too. I'll watch for it. Who should I return it to if I find it?"

"Just bring it to me. Thank you." As Faith returned to the stairs with Watson trailing, she thought about the notebook page Pierce had stuffed into his pocket and considered how many of the other authors would also be using such notebooks while at the manor.

Faith sighed once more. Those bits of paper in the vacuum could have been from anyone's notebook.

After supper, Faith curled under her grandmother's quilt in her favorite chair in front of the fireplace with a cup of hot tea while Watson sat on the back of the sofa watching whatever was lurking in the dwindling twilight outside the window.

Faith studied the printout of the woman in the lime-green dress, wondering again if she was grasping at straws to think Cybil had trekked down to the kennels after getting dressed up for the evening. Then again, Marlene had made the trip to the kennels in a dress and heels. It wasn't a difficult walk if the ground was dry.

But could Cybil's envy of Pierce's success be so deep that she'd lash out at Tara for choosing to profile Pierce over her in the article?

The phone rang, jolting her out of her thoughts.

It was Eileen. "As promised, I'm calling to let you know what I learned about the group's photographer. Jonathan Newell is a member of the horror writers group, but I couldn't find any other connection between him and Tara."

"I'm glad to hear it."

"Yes, but then I wondered something. What if Jonathan is close to Pierce or Cybil or Nolan? Perhaps he told one of them where Tara would be hanging out the night she died."

"And did you find any connections?"

"Yes, several," Eileen replied, and Faith could hear the satisfaction in her aunt's voice. "By day, Jonathan is a crime scene photographer. By night, he pens his novels. He hasn't found a publisher for any of them yet, but Nolan is his agent."

"Interesting."

"There's more. Jonathan photographed images on the covers of Pierce's last two books."

"Would Pierce have been involved in that process?" Faith asked.

"Not typically, but apparently Pierce requested him. Pierce also frequently taps Jonathan for crime scene information."

"So Jonathan could have casually mentioned having seen Tara and Cybil setting up the prank to either Nolan or Pierce, unaware of what either man might do with the information," Faith theorized.

"Earlier we talked about Pierce writing the note himself to deflect suspicion. Do you still think he did?"

Faith shrugged even though her aunt couldn't see her. "I don't want to dismiss any possibilities."

The metallic *clunk* of Faith's lion's head door knocker drifted through the cottage. "I have to go. Someone's at the door."

"Okay. I'll talk to you later."

After disconnecting, Faith set down her phone and her half-full cup of tea, then hurried to the door and opened it.

Wolfe smiled. "Sorry to drop by so late. Am I disturbing you?"

"No, not at all." She smiled in return and backed into the cottage, beckoning him in. "Do you have time for a cup of tea?"

"I'd love one. Thank you." He toed off his shoes and removed his coat.

"Have a seat by the fire, and I'll bring it in." When Faith returned to the living room with a cup of tea for him and a couple of chocolate chip cookies on the saucer, Wolfe was sitting on the sofa and dutifully giving Watson a thorough tummy rub.

"I can see he has you wrapped around his little paw," Faith teased.

Wolfe's smile brightened the room. "Petting animals is supposed to be good stress relief."

Faith sat down in her favorite chair again. "I imagine you could do with some stress relief. Worrying about the police investigation into Tara's death and Pierce's apparent death threat were extra stressors you didn't need on top of today's conference call."

"At least I know I can count on you and Marlene to watch out for the manor's best interests." Wolfe took a sip of tea.

"Of course."

"By the way, Chief Garris got back to me on the background check of our bookdealer, Ronald Adams."

"And?" Faith picked up her teacup and took a drink.

"You were right. Several would-be clients have accused him of burglarizing their homes soon after he paid them visits to show his wares."

"Oh no. Has he ever been convicted?"

"So far the police haven't been able to prove any of the allegations," Wolfe said. "He must be getting someone else to break in and handle the selling of the stolen goods. At one point he was also investigated for laundering money for organized crime, but again nothing could be proved."

Faith almost fumbled her teacup. "Tara wrote an article connected to organized crime."

Wolfe shook his head. "I think it's more plausible that someone at the retreat targeted Tara than to imagine Ronald Adams somehow securing the drug from the kennels and coming upon her at a conveniently secluded moment without anyone noticing him."

"I agree. But does anyone pay much attention to what others are doing? Staff probably would have assumed he was a guest, and guests might have assumed he was staff."

Wolfe held Faith's gaze with what looked like admiration. "I have to admit the same thing had occurred to me. I suggested to the chief that Ronald could have been a hired gun to silence Tara and that Pierce's death threat could be unconnected—someone taking advantage of a bad situation to spook him."

"What did he say?"

"Garris called the detective in charge of the case Tara reported on and alerted him to the possible connection. And to cover all his bases, he's given a copy of Ronald's photograph to his officers so they can watch out for him at tomorrow's signing in case he shows up."

"That's reassuring anyway."

"Are there any other developments at the manor I should know about?"

"Yes, just a moment." Faith retrieved the image she'd printed that afternoon and showed it to Wolfe. Then she filled him in on her theories and her exchange with Pierce over the notebook page.

Wolfe chuckled. "You've certainly got pluck."

Suddenly Faith didn't feel quite so embarrassed about pressing Pierce to let her examine the paper.

Wolfe asked to see the rest of the images on her computer. "Did you notice some of the pictures are missing?"

"How can you tell?"

He pointed out the number of the image on the screen, then advanced to the next one and the next one. "See? That one skipped two numbers."

"Jonathan must have deleted the photos that didn't turn out."

"Or the ones he didn't want you to see."

16

Faith slept restlessly, her mind rehashing Wolfe's remark about Jonathan deleting photos he didn't want her to see.

She woke up extra early and made coffee. As she waited for it to brew, she filled Watson's dishes and considered her conversation with Jonathan. He hadn't seemed concerned or suspicious when she asked him for the photos. In fact, he'd made a joke.

She sighed. But maybe it had been an act. Or perhaps he had felt confident, knowing she wouldn't see anything he didn't want her to.

After a light breakfast, Faith showered and got dressed. When she walked to the front door, she noticed the photo she'd printed sitting on an end table and tucked it into her pocket. "I'm going to the manor now," she called to Watson.

The cat raced out between her feet.

"Don't get into any mischief," Faith told him. "Once I finish setting up for the book signing, I'm heading into town for church."

She squinted in the direction Watson had taken off, but she couldn't see him. Turning toward the manor, she yelped at the sight of a pumpkin-headed scarecrow in her path with a hatchet in its head. With a killer at large, the thought of someone getting this close to her cottage long enough to erect it was far creepier than the maimed scarecrow itself.

Faith peered ahead to ensure there weren't any more surprises waiting for her in the Victorian garden between her house and the manor. Seeing none, she hurried along the path and slipped in through the front door. She was so early the front desk clerk wasn't in yet, and from how quiet the manor sounded—with blessedly no horror-themed music playing—she suspected most of the guests were taking advantage of the late breakfast to sleep in.

Faith proceeded to the gallery to ensure everything was ready for the afternoon's public event. Pierce was scheduled to deliver the main speech, and then there would be a book signing for all the authors.

Since they were expecting a large turnout, Marlene had asked the staff to set out the signing tables in front of the long line of windows and French doors, so fans could enjoy the beautiful ocean views while they waited to meet their favorite authors.

Faith covered each table with the requested black tablecloth and added signs identifying the authors. She kept it simple because Cybil had told her that many of the authors would bring their own decorations for their tables.

"You're here early."

Faith startled and turned to see Wolfe standing there. "I wanted to make sure we're ready for the book signing."

"It looks good. I'm sure the authors will be pleased." Wolfe glanced at his watch. "Chief Garris said that two officers will be here by eight to secure the area. They'll patrol the manor and grounds during the event."

"That's a relief. Do you think the murderer will try to get to Pierce?" She shivered at the prospect, even though she still wondered if the note had been a ruse on his part.

Before Wolfe could answer, a panicked shriek sounded from the second story and echoed off the gallery's marble floor and walls.

"What was that?" Faith asked.

"It sounded as if it came from one of the guest rooms." Wolfe ran for the stairs.

Faith followed him.

Upstairs, half a dozen bleary-eyed guests, still in their nightclothes, stood outside the Arthur Conan Doyle Suite.

"That's Pierce's room." Faith's heart dropped. Had the killer already struck?

"The scream came from in there," one of the guests told Wolfe. "But no one's answering the door."

Wolfe pounded on the door. "Mr. Baltimore, are you all right? Please open up."

A faint moan drifted out, and Faith breathed a grateful prayer of thanks.

Wolfe pulled his key ring from his pocket and unlocked the door. "Mr. Baltimore, I'm coming in to check on you." He turned to the other guests and said, "Stay back, please," then pushed inside.

The crowd reluctantly obeyed.

"Faith, get him some water," Wolfe called out through the open doorway.

Faith squeezed past the guests and entered the suite. She noticed a pitcher of water and a couple of glasses on a small table. She poured a glass, then approached the author.

Pierce was sitting up in bed, trembling uncontrollably, his skin ashen. Yet nothing in the room appeared disturbed. The antique Victorian desk in the corner, with its old forensic science books, magnifying glass, and test tubes, provided no clues.

She regarded the portrait of Sir Arthur Conan Doyle's most famous detective with his pipe and deerstalker cap. It hung perfectly straight on the wall, overlooking the room as if Sherlock Holmes might step out of the picture at any moment and deduce what had happened.

Faith offered the water to Pierce. He declined, so she set it down on the nightstand.

Wolfe held Pierce's wrist, checking his pulse. "What happened? Do you want us to call a doctor?"

Pierce raised a clenched hand and slowly opened his fingers, revealing two quarters. "These were on my eyes when I woke."

At the doorway, someone gasped.

Wolfe walked over to the door. "Please give Mr. Baltimore his privacy." He waved the guests away and shut the door, then turned back to Pierce. "I take it the coins mean something."

"It's an old superstition," Pierce said, his voice shaky. "Coins were placed on dead people's eyes so others wouldn't see their own deaths in the deceased's eyes. I wrote about it in my latest book."

"You didn't hear anyone come into your room? Or feel the coins placed on your eyes?" Wolfe asked, his voice betraying a hint of disbelief.

Pierce clutched his sheets and shook his head. "I always take a sedative to help me sleep."

"Just one?" Faith was surprised it would knock him out that soundly.

"Yes." Anger barreled into Pierce's tone. He balled his hands into fists. "I'm sure this is Cybil's doing."

Thinking of the incriminating photo she'd tucked into her pocket before leaving the cottage that morning, Faith glanced at Wolfe.

His frown suggested he might be recollecting the photo too.

"She ought to be kicked out for breaking into other guests' rooms," Pierce ranted. "This is tantamount to assault. If I had a weaker heart, I could have died of fright."

Faith went over to the door and examined the lock. "Did you turn the dead bolt before retiring?" There were no telltale signs the lock had been picked.

"Of course!"

Faith sent Wolfe a worried glance. Whoever did this either had the assistance of a staff member with a key, had stolen one, or was very good at breaking into places.

Watson jumped onto Pierce's bed.

Pierce recoiled. "How did that cat get in here?" he demanded.

"I'm sorry," Faith said. "He must have snuck past me when I came in."

Pierce shooed Watson off the bed.

Watson snatched something from the bedside table and then scrambled beneath the bed.

Faith bent down to try to coax him out.

But Watson backed into the corner out of her reach, a memo-size piece of paper in his mouth.

"What do you have there?" Faith asked him. "Come on. Let me see."

The cat dropped it and held it down with his paw, not budging.

"Can you reach him from that side?" she asked Wolfe.

Pierce bounced up and down on the bed, apparently figuring he'd scare Watson out.

It worked. Watson bolted out the other side of the bed.

Wolfe snagged him. He opened the room's door and gently set Watson in the hall.

Faith rounded the bed to try and reach the paper Watson had left behind.

"Is it true?" Marlene asked as she marched into the room. "A guest came to me blathering about someone breaking into Mr. Baltimore's suite and putting coins on his eyes."

"Yes." Wolfe's voice sounded as stern as Faith had ever heard it. "I want to talk with Ms. Crypt. Please take her to your office, and I'll be down shortly."

"Yes sir," Marlene said, then turned and left.

Wolfe shut the door once more.

Faith had to crawl halfway under the bed to reach the paper. She scooted back out and set it on Pierce's night table next to the monogrammed case holding his cell phone. Then she caught sight of what the note said. *I know what you did.*

Faith turned to Pierce. "What did you do?"

"What?" Pierce's tone had grown cold and impatient.

Faith showed him the note. "My cat grabbed this from your night table."

Pierce snatched it from her and crumpled it into a ball. "Nothing."

"Did you kill Tara?" Faith asked softly.

"Don't be ridiculous," he growled. "I only murder people in books."

"Faith." Wolfe gestured to the door. "We need to go and let Mr. Baltimore get dressed." To Pierce, he said, "We'll get to the bottom of this intrusion, and I assure you it won't happen again."

"Right. You also assured me I'd be safe here." Pierce held up the coins. "Whoever put these on my eyes could have just as easily plunged a knife through my heart." His hands trembled once more. "You can tell Cybil that she carried her little jokes too far this time. I'm going home."

"No," Faith blurted out. "I mean, what's the harm in staying a few more hours? Your fans are so looking forward to seeing you. Do you really want them all left to Cybil?"

Pierce snorted. "That was probably her plan all along. Get me to back out at the last minute so it would be too late for the fans to be notified."

Wolfe waited for Faith at the door, then urged Pierce to lock it behind them.

"I'm wondering if he might be right about Cybil," Faith admitted as they walked toward the stairs. "At first I thought the whole thing was an act, because I find it hard to believe he wouldn't feel coins being put on his eyes. Not to mention that they would stay on. I roll over at least half a dozen times in the night—don't you?"

"I suspect so, yes," Wolfe answered. "But why would he lie?"

"The same reason I've toyed with the suspicion he'd written the threatening note, especially given his reaction to Officer Tobin's questioning yesterday—to divert suspicion from himself in Tara's death."

"But you don't think that now?"

"Did you see the way he reacted to the note Watson found?"

Wolfe nodded. "I think it was the first time he'd seen it."

"I got that impression too. Which means someone else had been in the room at some point."

Wolfe started descending the stairs. "Let's hear what Cybil has to say about it."

By the time they reached Marlene's office in the basement, the assistant manager was already confronting Cybil.

"It wasn't me," Cybil claimed, appearing more than a little disturbed by the details. She shifted her gaze to Faith, then Wolfe. "I swear it wasn't me."

"Pierce said he'd written about the superstition in his latest book." Wolfe walked over to the desk and casually leaned against it, then refocused on Cybil and waited.

Cybil audibly gulped. "I don't know what you expect me to say."

"How about starting with the truth?" Wolfe said.

Faith pulled out the printed photo of Cybil wearing the lime-green dress. "And while you're at it, you can also tell us why you visited the kennels before Tara's murder."

"What?" Cybil took the picture and studied it. "I didn't go to the kennels. I was chasing one of the plastic tombstones the wind had picked up." She pointed to a gray blob on the ground ahead of her in the picture.

Wolfe raised an eyebrow at her skeptically.

"I'm telling the truth," Cybil insisted. "I didn't go into Pierce's room or to the kennels."

"But you know who did," Faith said.

She flinched and dropped her gaze. "I have a suspicion."

"Spit it out," Marlene ordered. "Is it that woman you asked me to hire?"

"You mean Carrie?" Faith asked since Carrie was the only new hire in over a month.

Marlene folded her arms across her chest. "Yes, only that's not her real name. I assumed they dubbed her that because she was going to reenact a scene from the Stephen King novel by the same name."

At the admission, Faith spun toward Cybil. "Is she Susan?"

"Who's Susan?" Marlene demanded.

"A writer Pierce Baltimore once mentored, then cast aside," Faith explained. "Tara recognized her. But no one else seemed to, although I sensed Pierce might have yesterday afternoon. He did a double take after glancing at her, but when I asked him if he recognized her from somewhere, he dismissed the notion."

Wolfe shifted his attention to Cybil. "Is Faith right?"

"Yes. She changed her hair color and style and stopped using makeup."

"She told me that no one notices the help," Faith added.

"But even so, I was pretty stunned that Tara was the only one who recognized her," Cybil admitted.

"You knew Tara recognized her?" Faith studied Cybil, wondering how far she would have gone to ensure Tara didn't foil their plans for the weekend.

"Susan told me. So when Tara and I were working out the animated topiary prank, I explained to her why Susan was incognito and asked her not to give Susan away."

"And Tara said no?" Faith asked.

"What?" Cybil jerked back, clearly aghast at the implication behind the question. "No, she thought it was funny that we'd planned some gags to bring Pierce down a few rungs. She agreed that the man considers himself utterly entitled."

"Did Susan get that message?" Faith asked.

"Yes," Cybil said. "I told her I'd talk to Tara and that everything would be fine."

"Did she believe you?" Wolfe asked.

The muscle in Cybil's cheek twitched. "I don't know."

"We need a straight answer," Wolfe persisted. "If Susan feared Tara would out her, was she capable of silencing her?"

Cybil covered her mouth, her gaze shifting to the door. "Maybe. Susan's really not malicious, but sometimes she loses control of her emotions. I mean, she has no control over them. It's a medical condition."

"You were there when one of the guests told me about that," Faith told Cybil. "But you dismissed it, saying it was simply rude behavior."

Cybil huffed. "I had to pretend like I'd never heard of Susan or her condition before. Though I truly believe that Pierce's shunning her because of something she has no control over was totally juvenile."

"You covered up for Susan after Tara's death," Faith accused.

"You ripped the page from Tara's notebook. How did you even know about it?"

"Just before Pierce came downstairs with the threatening note, I overheard Ruth tell you she had some questions about people Tara had made notes on since she arrived at the manor," Cybil explained. "I figured Susan was probably one of the people mentioned in Tara's notes."

"How did you get the notebook away from Ruth long enough to steal the page?" Marlene asked.

Cybil stared at the floor. "I snuck up to her room while everyone was waiting for the police. Ruth forgot to lock the door." She looked up. "But I didn't take the page because I thought Susan killed Tara. I just didn't want her cover blown."

"So that's the real reason why you asked me to hire Susan," Marlene said. "To make it easier to pull your pranks."

"Yes," Cybil admitted. "And it didn't take much convincing for Susan to accept the position. I knew she was between jobs and could use the money, and I thought she'd appreciate the chance for a little payback."

"What if Susan's idea of payback is more extreme than yours?" Wolfe said.

Again the twitch in Cybil's cheek telegraphed her uneasiness. "Susan wanted Pierce to pay for what he did, but it was only through the jokes. I don't believe she planned to hurt him physically."

"She wanted him to pay for humiliating her," Faith clarified.

"No, for plagiarizing her stories."

Faith couldn't help but gape at her. "Are you serious?" She recalled Susan's stunned reaction to Nolan's claim that one of his contestants had plagiarized Pierce's work.

"Yes, she showed me some of the stories on her laptop. Pierce hadn't copied them verbatim, but he'd used many of the same ideas."

"How do you know it wasn't her copying him?" Wolfe asked.

"Because of the file dates. They were all started well before Pierce began writing his manuscript."

"But Pierce mentored Susan," Faith reasoned. "Isn't it possible he showed her the notes for his latest book? Or that she stole a peek at them while visiting his home?"

Cybil frowned. "I guess it's possible."

Faith met Wolfe's gaze. "Susan had been in the library before the bookcase incident and then came running in afterward. She could have pocketed the doorstop I suspect was used to destabilize the bookcase. Like the other writing group members, she would have known exactly where Pierce would sit."

"What about the threatening note?" Cybil demanded. "Susan didn't slip that in his room. She still had it on her. There has to be someone else here who has it in for Pierce."

"Or Susan put her own copy of the note under the door to have even more fun playing with Pierce's mind." Faith hoped that psychologically tormenting the man was as far as Susan was willing to go.

"What exactly did Susan say she planned to do at this afternoon's event?" Wolfe asked Cybil.

"Play out Pierce's worst fear by doing what turned him against her in the first place."

"Which was?"

"Susan plans to show up at the book signing as herself to totally unnerve him. She believes he'll be paranoid that she'll embarrass him again. She'll laugh during his speech in the most inappropriate spot. Then she will accuse him of plagiarizing her stories."

The door burst open, revealing a fuming Pierce. "It's a lie!"

17

Faith, Wolfe, Cybil, and Marlene all swung around to face Pierce standing at the office door.

"I'm a best-selling author with more than five million books in print," Pierce declared. "No one will believe I plagiarized that ridiculous woman's stories. Did she sneak into my room last night?" He zeroed in on Cybil. "I suppose you put her up to it, didn't you?"

When Cybil didn't respond, Pierce glowered at Wolfe. "I trust you plan to fire that woman on the spot and ban her from the premises."

"I can assure you that we will take appropriate action," Wolfe answered evenly.

Pierce sneered at Cybil. "Next time you see Susan, tell her if she utters those lies in public she'd better be able to afford a good lawyer, because she's going to need one. And by the way, you can forget about me being at the book signing."

Cybil smirked. "You're afraid she'll show up?"

"I will personally watch for her and ensure she's escorted from the premises if she makes an appearance," Marlene promised.

"I plan to find her and get to the bottom of this long before she gets that chance," Wolfe said.

"You wouldn't want to disappoint your readers by skipping out on your speech and the book signing," Faith reminded Pierce, giving him a way to agree that would let him save face.

"Fine," Pierce spat out. "I'll be there. But only because I don't want to let my readers down."

"Susan has the day off," Marlene said. "So where is she now?"

Cybil shrugged. "I don't know. Perhaps she's at home."

"What's her address?" Wolfe asked.

Marlene looked it up on her computer, wrote it on a piece of paper, and handed it to Wolfe.

Leaving Marlene and Cybil to keep watch for Susan at the manor, Faith and Wolfe headed out to his car to track her down at her apartment.

Faith spotted Ruth walking in the garden and steered Wolfe in a different direction to the garage, hoping Ruth wouldn't notice them. Faith wanted to hear Susan's side of the story before she talked to Ruth.

"We can't tell Ruth yet," Faith whispered to him under her breath. "She might jump to the same assumptions we did. And act on them."

Wolfe nodded, but his agreement didn't assuage the guilt churning in Faith's gut.

"Don't worry," Wolfe said, opening the car door for her. "Once Susan has told us her side of the story, we'll fill Ruth in."

Faith sighed. "I can't believe Susan is capable of murder or even the tricks against Pierce for that matter. She seems too timid."

"But don't forget that even the sweet gray-haired ladies at this retreat conjure up gruesome horror stories."

Faith shivered. "Good point."

"I appreciate your accompanying me," Wolfe said as they drove into Lighthouse Bay. "I know it falls well outside your job description."

"Of course. But are you sure we shouldn't be going straight to the police with what we've heard? If Susan killed Tara . . ." Faith inhaled a shaky breath. She didn't want to picture Susan capable of such a cold-blooded act. It seemed hard to believe that she had gone that far to protect her secret. All so she could exact revenge on Pierce.

"I want to hear her side of the story before I make that call too. Pierce clearly isn't the noblest guy around."

Faith snorted. "He doesn't even make it onto the scale."

"For that reason, I wouldn't be surprised to learn that Susan has a justified complaint against him, and I wouldn't want that disregarded simply because Cybil thinks the woman might be capable of murder."

"That's her building." Faith pointed to a large three-story house with cedar shingles.

Wolfe parked at the curb.

Faith consulted the number Marlene had written down. "Her apartment is on the ground floor." She led the way and then knocked.

A dark-haired woman about Susan's age opened the door, and Faith did a double take. Was this what Susan looked like? Could she really change her appearance that drastically?

"May I help you?" the woman asked. Her voice sounded nothing like Susan's or at least nothing like the woman she'd been pretending to be.

Faith was jolted out of her stunned stupor. "Is Carrie in?"

"No, she's at church this morning."

"Do you happen to know which one she attends?" Wolfe asked.

"The one on the corner, I think. Would you like to come in and wait for her?"

"No thank you," Wolfe said, then guided Faith back toward the car with a touch to the middle of her back.

"Maybe we should have stayed. We might have learned something from her," Faith protested once they were inside the car again.

"Or she might have been intending to keep us occupied long enough for her to alert Susan so she could get away."

"Good point. I didn't think of that."

Wolfe drove to the end of the block and parked in the nearly empty church parking lot. "Most of the people have already left."

A few groups stood in the lot chatting as others walked out the open front doors of the church.

Faith and Wolfe climbed out of the car and searched the crowd for Susan.

"I don't see her out here," Wolfe said.

"I'll try inside." Faith sidestepped a small group at the door and slipped into the building.

"Can I help you find someone?" asked a spry older gentleman gathering bulletins from the pews.

"I'm looking for Carrie." Faith described her, but at the same time she wondered if she might have already transformed back to Susan.

"Yes, I remember her. She hurried out right at the end of the service. Said she had a special date."

Faith thanked him and rushed outside to tell Wolfe.

Wolfe dug in his pocket for his phone. "I'll inform Marlene in case 'special date' is Susan's code for messing with Pierce. Then we can drive around town to see if we can find her at any of the restaurants."

Visiting all the restaurants in Lighthouse Bay took longer than they expected. No one remembered seeing her, and despite driving up and down every street in town, they never spotted her car.

"Maybe we should check her apartment one more time," Faith suggested.

"We can do that," Wolfe said, "but then I think we'd better get back to the manor in case she's already there putting her plan into action. She might be stealthy enough to avoid even Marlene's eagle eye."

"Good idea. If she changed her appearance again, I doubt that anyone would recognize her. In fact, until her roommate spoke, I was wondering if she was Susan."

When they reached Susan's apartment, her roommate was walking out the door. "No, she hasn't been back. She probably got called to work. I'm sorry, but I've got to run now." With that she sprinted off.

Wolfe chuckled. "I didn't think she meant it literally."

Faith's phone beeped, and she read a text from Eileen. "Oh, wait," she said to Wolfe as they returned to his car. "Can we stop by my aunt's before we head back? She thinks she's figured out Pierce's secret."

"Absolutely." Wolfe waited for her to buckle up, then made a

U-turn. "Perhaps she's found proof that he plagiarized Susan's stories like she claims."

Eileen had her front door open and was waving them inside even before Wolfe turned the car off.

"Whatever the secret, she can't wait to tell us," Wolfe said as they practically jogged up the sidewalk.

Eileen led the way to her dining room table. "Look at this." She showed them Tara's article and pointed to the passage where Pierce talked about burning a boat in the name of research. "I found which novel that research is for."

"Which one?" Faith asked, skimming the passage.

Eileen pulled up one of Pierce's book covers on her laptop. "Then I figured out roughly when his manuscript would have been due to his publisher, and I searched for arson reports on boats from several months before that."

Faith scanned the titles on her aunt's Internet browser tabs. "What did you find?"

"An arson in a little town off the Georgia coast that matched the description of the town in Pierce's book, right down to the library overlooking the marina."

"So his secret is that he was charged with arson?" Wolfe asked.

"No." A shadow crossed Eileen's eyes. "It's much sadder and darker than that. Someone died in the fire. But the police were never able to identify the arsonist."

Faith gasped. "Who died?"

"A young runaway who'd been sleeping on the boat."

"And you think Pierce is responsible?" Wolfe said.

Eileen nodded. "It would explain the note Tara received, accusing her of whitewashing scum. I'm sure the police could locate credit card statements that place Pierce in the area around the time of the arson. He writes in great detail about a couple of places his character frequented in town."

"Tara might not have realized what Pierce did until after writing the article," Faith speculated. "Maybe someone who recognized the town in his book and knew the boy figured it out after reading her article, then urged her to set the record straight."

"Yes," Eileen continued. "If Tara confronted Pierce about what she'd learned that morning you saw them arguing, it would have given him plenty of motive to silence her."

"So who wants to kill Pierce?" Wolfe asked.

"He could have fabricated the threat as a smoke screen," Faith said.

Eileen closed her laptop. "You don't think he's in danger?"

"I think he's probably in danger of acute embarrassment from Susan's plans to crash the event today," Faith said. "But right now I'm more worried about what he might do to her if he sees her."

"Right. We'd better get back to the manor." Wolfe turned to Eileen. "Can you take this information to the police and explain it to them?"

"I sure will. But don't let Pierce know you're onto him. He's killed enough people already."

The cat padded after the human who'd shooed him off the bed earlier that morning. His stomach grumbled. He hoped his person would pick up more tunaroons from that store in town while she was gone. Earlier he'd seen her drive off with the nice man who lived on the top floor of the manor and always greeted him with an affectionate rub.

The human sauntered into the kennels, and one of the dogs started barking and whining.

The cat hung back. He couldn't understand why the dogs got so excited when their humans came to snap a lead on their neck and take them for a walk. It was so undignified. He would sooner crawl into a hole than traipse around the grounds on the end of a leash.

A thud and a muffled cry jolted the cat out of his thoughts. The noise sounded as if it had come from the kennels. He dashed over and was relieved to see the door was open a crack.

The cat slipped inside.

18

Faith's breath caught at the sight of Marlene rushing out of the manor to meet their car.

"Have you seen Susan?" Faith asked.

"No. And Pierce went to the kennels over an hour ago to take his dog for a quick walk. But he hasn't returned." Marlene checked her watch. "People will start arriving for his speech and the book signing in half an hour."

"Did you call down to the kennels to find out if they noticed which way he walked?" Wolfe asked.

"I did, but there's no answer. I was about to send one of the staff out to search for him."

"Is his car still here?" Faith asked. If the author had made a run for it, he had to know the police wouldn't be far behind.

"Yes," Marlene said impatiently.

"We'll drive to the kennels and see if we can find him," Wolfe said. "Text me if you see Susan or if Pierce returns."

Marlene nodded.

"Is Cybil inside?" Faith asked her.

"Yes, I believe so. She said she was going up to her room to change for the book signing."

"When was that?"

"It was about half an hour ago." Marlene spun around and hurried up the steps.

"Why did you ask about Cybil?" Wolfe said as he turned down the driveway that led to the kennels. "Are you having doubts that Pierce is our man?"

"I don't like that Pierce is missing. Eileen's theory makes total sense—if it's true. But even if it is, there's clearly more going on. And we only have Cybil's word about Susan's plans to humiliate Pierce." Faith peered out the windshield. "What if they really had something totally different planned?"

"Cybil could have told Susan that we were looking for her."

"Exactly. Then decided she would have to take care of Pierce."

As soon as Wolfe parked next to the kennels, Watson came barreling out of the building and headed straight for Faith.

"Somebody missed you," Wolfe remarked.

Faith smiled as she scooped up the cat and gave him a cuddle. "He thinks I'll have a tunaroon for him. I usually buy some when I go to town." To Watson, she said affectionately, "Are you teasing the dogs again?"

He gazed at her innocently.

She set him on the ground and attempted to follow Wolfe into the kennels.

But Watson twined around her legs, meowing loudly, and almost tripped her.

Faith picked him up again. "I need you to be good, okay? We have to find Pierce right now." She carried him inside the building.

Wolfe met her at the office door. "Annie says she saw Pierce heading down here when she went for her break about an hour ago, but when she returned twenty minutes later, his dog was still here."

"Well, I'm pretty sure Pierce wouldn't have skipped town without Hannibal," Faith said. "He seems devoted to his dog."

Watson wriggled out of Faith's arms and jumped to the floor. He scurried away, and Faith and Wolfe followed him to the kennel that housed Pierce's border collie.

Hannibal jumped at the door again and again, barking wildly.

Annie walked over and tried to calm him.

"Does Hannibal do that a lot?" Faith asked the young attendant.

"No, he just started this afternoon." She flipped her thick brown braid over her shoulder.

Faith noticed her cat pawing at the pile of wood chips next to the dog's kennel and walked over to see what he'd found. She picked up the object and instantly recognized the monogrammed case. "This is Pierce's phone."

Wolfe knelt down and studied the spot where Watson had been pawing. "It almost looks as if something—or someone—was dragged from here. See how the sawdust has been brushed clear of the cement in two parallel lines?"

Faith's heart skipped a beat. She scanned the floor for more evidence, then pointed to a scuff a few feet away. "There's another one." Faith pressed her hand to her now-pounding heart. "What if Susan was waiting for him in here and he attacked her?"

"Check the storage rooms, the stalls, the cupboards, anywhere he might have hidden her," Wolfe told Annie, pulling out his phone. A few seconds later, he had Marlene on the other end. "Can you give me Susan's cell phone number?" He disconnected and tapped it in.

Seconds later, the faint sound of the theme music from *Psycho* momentarily played.

"That's Susan's ringtone," Faith said. She remembered hearing it in the library when Susan had been skulking around the stacks.

It sounded again. Louder this time.

Susan walked around the corner and stopped in her tracks when she saw them.

Faith looked her up and down. Susan appeared fine, and there wasn't a speck of dirt or any wood shavings on her clothes. "You're okay."

"Yes," Susan said, peering at Faith oddly. "Are you?"

Thrown by her seeming obliviousness, Faith stared at her. Why hadn't security alerted them she was openly strolling the grounds? And if Susan was fine, where was Pierce?

"What are you doing here?" Wolfe demanded.

Susan shrank from his abrupt tone. "It's my day off. I came for the book signing. I'm a huge horror buff. Ask Faith."

"The book signing is up at the manor," Wolfe reminded her.

"Yeah, but they aren't starting for a bit, so I thought I'd come down and visit with Hannibal. I've always wanted a dog, but my parents wouldn't let me have one. Now I live in an apartment where pets aren't allowed." Susan walked over to Pierce's dog and let herself into his kennel. "How are you, boy? Miss me?"

Hannibal instantly calmed and wagged his tail. Of course he would know her, if she'd spent a lot of time with Pierce before he excised her from his life.

"He seems to know you," Faith baited.

Susan smirked. "Cybil already called to tell me you know who I am. She said you were trying to find me. And that they had orders to stop me from entering the manor."

"Is there anything you want to tell us?" Wolfe asked.

Susan slipped out of the dog's kennel and latched the gate. "I admit I pulled the coin prank on Pierce, and I know I'm probably fired for going into a guest's room when I shouldn't have."

"You think?" Faith said, though it was hardly her call.

"I'm not sorry," Susan said, lifting her chin. "Cybil said she told you what he did. Pierce deserves to be tormented. But I swear I have no intention of killing him. He's not worth the price I'd have to pay."

"Did you slide the note that said 'You're next' under his door?" Faith asked.

"It was a stroke of genius to substitute my own note for Cybil's, so I could produce hers to prove the note he'd found wasn't a joke." Susan beamed. "I'd never seen him so freaked out."

"What about the note on Pierce's bedside table?" Wolfe asked. "Did you leave that one too?"

Susan furrowed her brow. "No, I didn't leave any others."

Faith realized their earlier conclusion might have been backward. Pierce could have lost his phone while *being* attacked, not while *launching* one. Faith said, "The note said, 'I know what you did.'"

Susan laughed. "It sounds like me, but it wasn't. Maybe Cybil left it."

"Where's Pierce now?" Wolfe asked.

"How should I know? You've barred me from going into the manor. I imagine he's getting ready for his public appearance."

Faith scrutinized her expression. Did Susan honestly not know Pierce was missing?

Wolfe called Marlene again. "We've got Susan. Have you checked Pierce's room for him?"

"Just now." Her frantic response was so loud that Wolfe held the phone away from his ear. "He's not here. No one has seen him since he left for the kennels."

"We'll keep looking." Wolfe tapped off the phone and led the way outside. When they neared his car, he squinted at the horizon. "I think we should call the police. I thought Garris might come on his own after Eileen shared her theory with him."

"What theory?" Susan asked.

Faith hesitated. She had an uneasy feeling that Susan might be here only to distract them. A decoy. "Why did you kill Tara?" Faith blurted out.

Shock transformed Susan's expression. "I didn't!"

Wolfe cocked his head, studying her.

"You've got to believe me!" Susan wailed. "I would never kill anyone. Not even Pierce. Tara was a good friend and always nice to me. I hated pretending I wasn't who she thought I was." She hugged herself. "I was glad when Cybil told her she'd been right about me."

"I didn't notice you cry after her body was found," Faith said, unwilling to be reeled in by another act. "If she was such a good friend—"

"But I wasn't supposed to know her," Susan interrupted. "Don't you see? I couldn't cry." She ducked her head. "And sometimes I have emotional reactions I can't control. Inappropriate ones. I was terrified that would happen."

Annie and a stable hand ran over to them. "We've searched every inch of the stables. Mr. Baltimore is not here."

"I'm calling Garris," Wolfe said. He took out his phone.

"What's going on?" Susan asked.

Faith's gaze skittered over her pristine clothes—not the clothes of someone who'd just dragged away a body. "We found evidence suggesting someone might have been in a tussle with Pierce," she explained. "We thought you were waiting for him. But apparently someone else really is after him."

Susan gasped. "I'm sorry for causing you so much trouble."

"Can you think of anyone else who might want to kill him?" Faith asked.

"I don't know." Susan wrung her hands. "He always got creepy fan mail. You might ask his publisher."

One of the guests sauntered by them and headed toward the kennels, a cigarette dangling from his lips.

"Sorry." Wolfe pointed to the *No Smoking* sign. "You'll need to finish that out here."

The guest mumbled an apology and shuffled away.

"That's it," Faith whispered. "The arson."

"What are you talking about?" Wolfe asked.

Her thoughts were miles away—in southern Georgia to be specific. "Who else would want to make Pierce pay?"

Understanding dawned in his eyes. "The arson victim's family."

"Exactly." Faith called Eileen. "What was the name of the arson victim? Were his parents still alive? Did he have any siblings?"

"His name was Andy Stephenson. According to his online obituary, he was survived by a mother, June, and an older brother, William."

"William," Faith repeated softly. "That's why Bill didn't give Tara his full name."

"Who's Bill?" Wolfe asked.

"The vet shadowing Midge. He's the victim's brother. His name is

Dr. William Stephenson. It couldn't be a coincidence. He treated Tara's cat and told her to call him Bill. He must have known she'd recognize who he was otherwise."

"She wouldn't recognize him on sight?" Wolfe asked.

"Not if he'd only ever corresponded with her. He must have figured out Pierce had killed his brother after he read Tara's article. If he didn't get anywhere with the police, maybe he urged her to expose him."

"Then he became angry when she wouldn't," Wolfe surmised.

Susan's eyes widened. "He had access to all the drugs!"

"And he knows how to use them and what they do," Faith added.

Wolfe asked Annie to check the medical supplies to see if anything else was missing since they were inventoried.

"I can't. I don't have a key," she said.

"Midge has them locked down now," Faith said, already dialing her friend's number.

Wolfe instructed Annie to ensure the lock hadn't been tampered with.

"Midge," Faith said the second the call connected, "where's Bill?"

"I assume he's on his way back to Martha's Vineyard. Why?"

"We think he's after Pierce. We suspect one of Pierce's research exploits killed Bill's younger brother."

Midge gasped. "You think Bill . . . ? I can't believe it. He never said a word—oh," she said as if suddenly remembering something significant.

"What is it?" Faith pressed. "Did he say something?"

"No, I was thinking it would explain why he dropped the vials. If he was trying to cover up the drugs he stole."

"Yes," Faith said. "And now Pierce is missing. We need to find them both before—"

"I'll try calling Bill," Midge interrupted. "If he doesn't answer, I'll drive by his B&B to see if I can spot his truck."

Wolfe obviously overheard what Midge had said, because he reached for Faith's phone. "Call us the second you locate him. Don't let on that you know anything about his brother's connection to Pierce. In fact, it would be better if you didn't engage him at all."

Faith took back the phone. "Could Bill have accessed any more drugs since you changed the locks?"

"Not unless he picked the lock. Marlene has the only other key."

"Good to hear. Okay, we need to start searching. Keep in touch with what you learn." Faith disconnected the call.

"If Bill planned to kill Pierce," Wolfe said, "he wouldn't have wanted to be seen at the manor today. He probably waited for Pierce at the kennels, knowing he'd come to walk his dog. But then where would he take him?"

"Are you guys talking about Dr. Bill?" Annie asked.

"Yes, have you seen him?" Wolfe said.

"No, but when we were searching the buildings, I noticed his black pickup parked behind the utility shed."

"He's still on the grounds somewhere," Faith said.

Watson twined around her legs.

"Not now, Watson. You go play."

"If it was my brother he killed," Susan said, "I'd want to put him through what he put my brother through."

Burn him in a boat? "Would Bill want to risk being seen by other boaters or people on shore?" Faith started toward the ocean.

Watson scampered around her legs, almost tripping her yet again. When she stopped, he meowed up at her.

Realizing he knew something, she squatted beside him. "What is it?"

Watson meowed again and bounded toward the kennels.

Faith sprinted after him with Wolfe and Susan on her heels.

At the door of the building, Watson glanced back at her.

"I'm right behind you," she told him.

Watson raced straight over to Hannibal's kennel.

As soon as Pierce's dog saw them, he went into another barking frenzy, throwing himself at the door.

Faith peeked inside the kennel. "Is there something in there?"

Watson pawed at the gate latch.

"Okay, okay, I'm looking," Faith said. She walked alongside the kennel, searching for a clue. "Do you see anything?" she asked the others.

Watson hooked his paw around the latch handle and yanked.

Hannibal slammed his front paws against the gate once more, and this time it swung wide open. The dog took off, straight down the center of the building and out the back door.

Watson followed him.

"That's it!" Faith exclaimed. "He wants us to follow the dog. He's probably picked up Pierce's scent."

Faith chased after them. Wolfe soon outpaced her and took up the lead behind Hannibal and Watson with Susan bringing up the rear. Branches lashed Faith as she ran at full speed to keep the animals in view. Even so, they began to lag behind the dog.

Faith caught up with Wolfe. "Do you think he's really on Pierce's trail?"

"Let's hope so," Wolfe said between labored breaths. "And that he keeps barking. I've lost sight of him."

Hannibal's barking suddenly ceased, followed by the sound of a splash.

"There's water out here?" Faith asked.

"A pond." Wolfe picked up speed.

A faint cry drifted through the trees. "No, go back! Get help, boy!"

"Is that Pierce?" Faith whispered.

Wolfe signaled for her to stay quiet, and they slowed to a silent walk.

Behind them, Susan veered to the left. "Pierce is tied up in an old rowboat in the middle of the pond," she hissed. She motioned them to a small break in the trees and pointed to the water visible through it.

Pierce's dog paddled frantically around the boat, struggling to climb in and nearly tipping it.

Bill wore a baseball cap pulled low and sat a stone's throw away from Pierce in another rowboat. "If you don't want to burn," he taunted, igniting a road flare and then tossing it toward Pierce's boat, "you can always throw yourself overboard."

Faith gasped. "He'll drown."

19

The sizzling red flare fell a couple of feet short of Pierce's boat and fizzled out in the water.

With the thick forest surrounding the pond, no one would have noticed the flare if Pierce's dog hadn't been able to track his master and lead them to him.

Bill pulled the cap off another flare.

"How are we going to stop him?" Faith whispered. "We don't have a way to get to him."

Wolfe quietly phoned Eban Matthews, a young gardener at the manor, and told him to bring the yacht's self-inflating life raft on the ATV to the old fishing pond and to have someone direct the police to their location.

"Help!" Pierce struggled to break free of his bindings while he attempted to discourage his dog from climbing over the side and tipping him to certain death.

Bill struck the flare against the scratch plate. "Are you ready to admit you torched the boat?"

"I don't know what you're talking about," Pierce said when the flare didn't ignite.

"This is like Pierce's last novel," Susan whispered. "They say your life flashes before your eyes when you drown. Do you think that's true?"

"We're not going to let him drown," Faith hissed.

Susan parted the leaves slightly and peeked through them at the unfolding scene. "They say if you rescue a drowning man, he'll hate you."

"Where do you get this stuff?" Faith asked. "Unless the victim wanted to be dead, it makes no sense."

Bill struck the flare again, and it erupted into a bright orange flame.

He raised it over the water and squinted toward Pierce, seemingly taking aim. He tossed the flare.

"Okay, yes, I did it!" Pierce screamed, ducking.

The flare landed dangerously close to Hannibal still paddling frantically next to the boat. The dog disappeared below the surface.

"I admitted it!" Pierce screamed. "I doused the boat with kerosene and ignited it with a flare. Please don't hurt my dog!"

"What makes you think I'm any different than you?" Bill snarled.

Hannibal resurfaced amidst the smoke now hovering over the water's surface from the doused flares.

"The dog will be okay," Susan whispered. "A victim always resurfaces three times before succumbing."

Faith bit back a retort. The young woman was seriously disconnected from reality. Bill was trying to set Pierce's boat on fire, and Susan was reciting old wives' tales.

"Did you hear my brother scream for help?" Bill went on angrily, lifting another unlit flare into view. "Did you even try to save him? Or did you watch from a distance, taking notes of the smells and sounds and tastes, while he burned to death in front of you?"

Pierce wrenched his arms and legs, causing the boat to rock wildly, as he struggled to break free of the ties binding his wrists and ankles. "I didn't know he was on the boat. I swear I didn't know."

"But you figured it out later, didn't you? When the news reported the runaway's death." Bill struck the flare. "And you didn't turn yourself in." He tossed the flare high in the air.

Faith and Carrie muffled gasps.

But the flare landed harmlessly in the water beyond the boat.

The dog yipped, frantically pawing at the boat.

"We can't wait any longer," Faith whispered.

Wolfe swept aside the leaves that had shielded them from view. "The game's over, Stephenson. The police are on their way."

Pierce uttered a prayer of thanks.

"The police are useless," Bill griped. "I told them months ago that Baltimore killed my brother. They laughed me out of the station."

Faith stepped forward. "We heard his confession. He can't get away with what he did now."

For a split second, Pierce looked as if he might protest. Then he glanced at the new flare in Bill's hand and seemed to think better of it.

"You bet he won't." Bill ignited the flare. But this time his toss went wide.

Was Bill deliberately missing to torture Pierce? Or did he just have terrible aim?

At the sound of an approaching ATV, Faith's racing heart slowed a fraction.

But then the engine changed pitch and stopped. "Mr. Jaxon?" Eban called through the trees. "The trees are too dense. I can't drive any farther. I'll have to carry the raft the rest of the way."

Wolfe raced over to help him.

The whimpering dog pulled himself halfway over the side of the boat, and Pierce had to fling himself to the opposite side to stop it from tipping.

Laughing, Bill tossed another flare.

"There isn't time to wait for the raft," Faith said to Susan. She shed her jacket and kicked off her shoes. "The boat's going to capsize, and Pierce will drown before they can reach him." Faith dived into the water.

"He isn't worth it," Bill called out.

Years of swimming lessons came back to her with the first few strokes. Faith stretched her arms and kicked harder, praying Bill wouldn't throw another flare before she reached the boat. It seemed so far away.

Putting her head down, Faith cut six strokes through the water between breaths. Her wet clothes dragged in the water, slowing her progress. The cold water sapped her energy. She pushed harder.

Hannibal paddled toward her and tried to climb on top of her. "Down, boy."

The dog licked her face.

"Good boy. You did great. You swim back now. Call him in!" Faith yelled to Susan.

"Here, Hannibal," Susan called. "Come on."

The dog whined at Pierce, then slowly headed toward the shore.

Faith finally made it to Pierce's boat. She slung her arms over the side to catch her breath. "Shift to the other side, so I don't tip the boat when I get in."

Pierce quickly obeyed.

Faith glanced at Bill. He sat watching them from his boat, which seemed closer. He held another unlit flare.

Drawing a deep breath, Faith gripped the edge of the boat. With a swift kick, she straightened her elbows and hoisted herself over the side of the boat. She plopped ungracefully into the bottom.

Wolfe crashed through the trees, towing a giant white barrel with Eban. "Help me get this in the water," he ordered.

Faith scrambled to gain her seat in the rowboat. "Quick. Turn so I can get your hands untied," she said to Pierce.

He twisted around and raised his tied arms as far as he was able.

"What's that smell?" Faith glanced at the bottom of the boat. "Are those rags soaked in what I think they are?" She tossed out a handful.

Bill heaved another flare. Only this one landed in the boat.

Faith screamed and tried to kick it out. But it bounced onto the remaining rags, and they burst into flames.

She ripped the last knot free from Pierce's wrists and flung herself back into the water.

When she resurfaced, Pierce was still in the burning boat working on the rope around his ankles.

"There's no time!" Faith reached over the side of the boat and hauled him out, his feet still bound.

As she reached over a second time to grab an oar to pull him with, Pierce seemed to panic. He grabbed her and dragged her under.

Splaying her palms, Faith tucked her chin and pushed up with all her strength to thrust herself even deeper. As she'd hoped, he let go. She swam farther away from him before clawing back to the surface. "Calm down," she ordered.

"Baltimore will kill you too," Bill warned. "He only cares about himself."

Faith ignored him. "Spread out your arms and float on your back," she instructed Pierce.

He flailed wildly for another few seconds, then finally relaxed into a dead man's float.

"That's it." She swam around to come in behind him. She had to give him credit. Without having his legs free to kick, it had to be unnerving to trust he wouldn't sink.

The boat was engulfed in flames, but one oar had slipped from its mount into the water. She grabbed hold of it to offer to him if he panicked again before Wolfe got to them with the raft.

Hannibal must have reversed direction when Pierce yelled, because the next thing she knew, the dog was trying to rest his upper body on Pierce's.

Pierce panicked, arms flailing once more.

Faith poked one end of the oar toward him. "It's okay. Grab hold."

Pierce pounced on the end and pulled it hand over hand, drawing her closer.

She immediately let go, but he was already too close. He yanked her under a second time.

Faith swallowed a mouthful of water. The circle of light at the pond's surface shrank with dizzying speed. Her life flashed before her eyes. *This is it. I'm going to die.*

She would *not* go gently into this good night. A burst of determination surged through her veins. She rammed the butt of her hand into Pierce's nose and fought her way back to the surface.

The instant she broke through to glorious air, Susan cried, "Oh no, that's two!"

Spotting Wolfe and Carrie rowing toward her, Faith filled her lungs with enormous gulps of air. "Knock it off, Susan! You're not helping!"

"Hang on, Faith!" Wolfe shouted. "We're coming." His powerful strokes quickly closed the distance between them.

But Pierce hadn't resurfaced yet.

Faith plunged back under. Twisting around behind him, she clamped her arms under his armpits and kicked them both up for air. Out of the corner of her eye she noticed Hannibal veer toward them once more. "Call the dog," she said.

Wolfe summoned Hannibal.

"It's unlucky to rescue a drowning man!" Susan wailed.

Pierce's head jolted up and back, whacking Faith in the nose, and before she knew what was happening, Pierce had her under for the third time.

Fighting his iron grip, Faith struggled to kick back to the surface. She could see the silhouettes of Wolfe and Susan in the approaching raft. A life buoy on a rope slapped the water overhead. Her lungs burned as she fought to tear Pierce's fingers from around her arm.

Just when she thought she couldn't hold her breath another second, a second splash of water sounded.

Susan appeared and rammed her elbow into Pierce's head. He instantly released his grip, and Susan pushed Faith toward the life buoy.

The three of them resurfaced, and Pierce reached for Faith yet again.

There was a loud hiss, and a familiar paw, claws outstretched, sliced across Pierce's arm from the raft above.

Pierce yanked his arm away.

Wolfe hauled Faith onto the raft and rubbed her frigid arms.

Watson leaped into her lap and pressed himself against her body, seeming not to care that she was soaked.

Faith cuddled her cat. "I was afraid Susan might be proven right about going under three times before you drown," she quipped.

Wolfe peeled off his coat and wrapped it around her shivering body. "You're safe now."

"Pierce?" she asked breathlessly.

Wolfe shifted so she could see for herself.

Panic swelled her throat. The man was flailing uselessly and ignoring the life buoy Susan had shoved toward him from a safe distance away.

Bill jumped into the water and swam toward him.

"No!" Faith cried out.

Watson yowled.

Bill lifted Pierce's head above water. "I'm not going to let him die," he said. "I only wanted to teach him a lesson."

"Are you kidding me?" Faith shouted. "You doused rags in the bottom of his boat with gasoline."

Bill shook his head. "He had to think I'd let him burn or there was no point."

Treading water, Susan stared at Bill uncertainly.

Faith imagined Susan was wondering the same thing she was. Could they trust Bill not to shove Pierce under again the instant Susan climbed back onto the raft?

Bill hoisted Pierce into his own rowboat. "Come on," he said to Susan. "You can row him in."

Susan climbed into the boat.

"I'll swim." Bill took off for shore in the fastest front crawl Faith had ever seen.

"He's trying to get away," she said.

The police sirens sounded as if they were getting close, but the officers would still have more than a mile of trail to cover on foot.

"I doubt he plans to escape." Wolfe paddled after Bill toward shore. "If he wanted to, he would have taken off in his boat. I suspect he's realized too many people saw his attempt to kill Pierce. He must know that even if he managed to get away, he'd be on the run for the rest of his life."

"I hope you're right," Faith said, tugging Wolfe's coat tighter around herself.

"If I'm wrong, Eban will stop him."

Faith's gaze lifted to the other boat in time to see Susan pull Hannibal into it.

Pierce divided his time between coughing up pond water and fighting the bindings around his ankles while his dog frolicked around him, delirious with joy.

Susan, her wet hair dripping down her cheeks, her drenched clothes clinging to her limbs, propelled the boat in powerful, synchronized strokes, ignoring the boat's dramatic rocking from the dog's movements.

"Thank you for saving my life," Faith called across to her.

Susan shook her head as if she still couldn't quite believe it. "When I saw you go down for the third time, I knew that was it."

"But it's unlucky to rescue a drowning man," Faith teased. "Isn't that what you said?"

Susan glanced at Pierce and snorted. "I didn't do it for him. And I probably will regret saving *him*." She grinned at Faith. "But if you don't hate me for saving you, I might start to think you're right about there being nothing to the superstitions after all."

20

By the time their life raft reached the shore, Eban had Bill face-down on the ground and was tying his wrists together.

Wolfe jumped from the raft and yanked it farther onshore, then ushered Faith over to a nearby log and urged her to sit.

Watson's body pressed against her chest chased the chill from her bones. The cat rubbed his soft head against her chin and purred loudly.

"You're still shivering." Wolfe retrieved her jacket from the ground where she'd dropped it and wrapped it around her wet legs, then zipped his jacket to her chin over Watson. "Better?"

Faith nodded.

Wolfe helped Susan tow the rowboat onshore. In Pierce's rush to scramble out, he stumbled and fell into the shallows.

Hannibal eagerly splashed over to him and licked his face.

Pierce gave his dog an enormous hug. "Good boy. Thanks for helping them find me." Man and dog waded ashore together.

It was surprising to see how attached Pierce was to the animal when he was so aloof with people. Faith felt sorry for the dog. He obviously adored Pierce, and she had a feeling the man would end up behind bars for a long time. She hoped he had relatives who would take the dog until he got out again.

If he got out.

Wolfe helped Susan from Bill's boat, then passed Eban's jacket to her.

Susan huddled under it and shivered. "Do you think we can get a ride back on the ATV once the police get here?"

"Of course," Wolfe answered as he returned to the boat. He snatched up the rope that had bound Pierce's feet.

Faith glanced at the trees. What was taking the police so long?

She wanted to get out of these wet clothes and cozy up in front of her fireplace with a cup of hot tea.

"Thanks for saving me out there," Pierce said, shaking Faith's hand. "I'm sorry I panicked on you."

Faith nodded, her emotions toward him uncomfortably mixed after what he'd confessed.

Pierce also thanked Wolfe effusively.

"You're welcome," Wolfe said, then caught Pierce's hands and yanked them behind his back.

"Hey! What are you doing?"

Pierce's dog went into another barking frenzy.

"Quiet." Wolfe tied Pierce's wrists and sat him down with his back to a tree. "You confessed to murder. How do I know you won't try to make a run for it before the police arrive?"

"But I didn't do it," Pierce protested. "I said what he wanted to hear so he'd let me go."

Roaring, Bill rolled onto his side and up to his feet, his hands still bound behind his back.

Eban caught him by the elbow. "Easy."

"Right," Susan said, sarcasm dripping from her voice. "Just like you didn't plagiarize my stories. Or kill Tara."

"I didn't!" Pierce's cheeks blazed brighter than the flames that had almost engulfed him. "I never laid a hand on Tara."

A deeper chill shivered through Faith. This wasn't over. Short of a confession, the police might never be able to prove Pierce killed Tara.

Susan pinned Pierce with a glare that warned him to lie at his own risk. "Faith heard you arguing with Tara the morning she died. What was that about?"

He shook his head. "It was nothing. Tara overheard me talking to someone about my research exploits with a new writer, and she got mad. She said I was arrogant and I had to stop before someone else got hurt."

Susan's scowl intensified. "In other words, she knew your dirty little secret and you decided she needed to be silenced."

"What? No!" Pierce inhaled and straightened to his full height. "I told her she'd been misguided and assured her that if she printed lies about me, I'd sue her and her publisher."

"They aren't lies," Bill said. "Everyone here heard you confess."

Pierce shrugged. "Under duress. Last I heard, a confession under torture wasn't admissible in this country."

"Why you—" Bill lunged for him, but Eban stopped him.

Faith couldn't blame Bill. It made her sick how Pierce continued to deny what he'd seemingly done. But he was so cocky and egotistical that she suspected he honestly believed Tara wouldn't have dared cross him. And if he believed that, then why kill her? Maybe because he was also cocky enough to think he could get away with it?

"So you admit that Tara leveled accusations against you?" Susan reiterated.

"Sure." Pierce jutted his chin in Bill's direction. "He must have filled her head with them. But obviously neither of them had any proof, or I would have had that conversation with the police."

"You were there!" Bill shouted at Pierce. "I have B&B records and restaurant records to prove it. Eyewitnesses who saw you around the marina."

Faith shifted her attention to Bill. "Was it Tara's article that tipped you off that Pierce was responsible for the fire that killed your brother?"

He nodded.

"So why not take your evidence to the police?"

"I did. But they wouldn't listen to me."

"Did you ask Tara to go public with the information?" Faith asked.

"That's right."

"It must have angered you when she refused," Faith persisted.

Rage flared in Bill's eyes, but then he said calmly, "She claimed the evidence was too circumstantial. That her editor would never agree to print it."

"So you began plotting your own form of justice," Wolfe interjected.

"Yeah, I guess you could call it that." Bill glared at Pierce. "Since Baltimore was so *committed* to getting his details accurate, it seemed fitting that he should experience them firsthand."

"Were you the one who put the note that said 'I know what you did' on Pierce's night table?" Faith asked.

Bill laughed. "Is that where it ended up?" He smirked at Pierce. "That must have freaked you out, thinking I'd been in your room."

"Then how did it get on his night table?" Wolfe asked.

"I don't know," Bill replied. "I slipped it into his pocket when he was leaving the kennels."

"I always empty my pockets onto the night table before I change for bed," Pierce muttered. "Since I had a pounding headache last night, I didn't pay any attention to the stuff."

Keeping her tone conversational, Faith asked Bill, "Did Tara figure out what you were up to? Threaten to expose you?"

Bill snorted. "Not at all. She'd never met me. She didn't even have a clue that I was the one who'd asked her to expose Baltimore."

If that was true, then Bill would have had little motive to kill her. Faith recalled the day when Bill helped Midge treat Tara's cat. She'd certainly gotten the impression it was Tara and Bill's first meeting.

"Whose phone is that?" Eban asked, looking about for the source of the ringtone Faith hadn't noticed until that moment.

"That's mine." Faith patted the pockets of her coat sprawled over her legs and found her phone. Watson squirmed, and she unzipped Wolfe's jacket to let him scamper away as she answered the phone.

"The police said you found Bill," Midge said breathlessly.

"Yes, at a pond in the middle of the woods. The police are on their way."

The sound of approaching ATVs hummed through the trees.

"Good, because I've been to Bill's B&B and I found the smoking gun."

"What?" Faith glanced from Bill to the still-smoking rowboat he'd torched in the middle of the pond as she tried to make sense of what Midge meant.

Chief Garris burst through the trees. Officers Laddy and Tobin were right behind him.

"The police just got here," Faith said to Midge.

"Okay, I'll let you go and explain when you get back. Stay safe." Midge clicked off before Faith could protest.

Chief Garris scanned the group. "Does someone want to bring me up to speed?"

Wolfe helped Bill to his feet and handed him off to Officer Tobin. "This is Dr. Bill Stephenson. He kidnapped Pierce, bound him, and set him adrift in the pond, then proceeded to taunt him by throwing flares at the boat."

"I wasn't trying to kill him. I would have let him go eventually," Bill claimed, clearly hoping for clemency.

"You planted gas-soaked rags in the bottom of the boat," Faith reminded him. "You expect us to believe you thought he could survive them lighting up like an inferno?"

Bill scowled at her. "I was only pretending to try to hit the boat to scare him."

Faith motioned to the boat. "Then your aim is terrible."

"You've got to believe me," Bill said pleadingly to the chief. "I just wanted him to feel the terror he put my brother through."

Garris turned to Faith. "So your aunt's theory is true?" He shook his head and motioned Officer Laddy to take Pierce into custody as well.

"No!" Pierce protested, resisting Laddy's hold. "I just told the psycho what he wanted to hear so he'd stop throwing those flares at me."

"Don't believe him," Susan piped up. "He says he didn't plagiarize my stories either, but I can prove he's a liar."

Pierce glared at her. "Try it and my lawyer will make you regret it."

The chief looked to Faith as if she should be able to settle the dispute.

"I haven't seen her proof," Faith said. "But I did hear Pierce admit to dousing the abandoned boat with kerosene and tossing a flare to ignite it."

The chief's eyes widened. "What accelerant did he claim to use?"

"Kerosene." Faith turned to Wolfe for confirmation. "Is that what you heard?"

"Yes. I remember thinking why not gasoline, which would have been easier to come by and less difficult to track. But I suppose he didn't think anyone would try since he thought the boat was empty."

"Take him in," the chief said to Officer Laddy.

Pierce struggled against Laddy's hold. "You can't arrest me. You have no proof. The man was torturing me when I made that confession."

Officers Tobin and Laddy escorted Bill and Pierce through the trees toward the ATVs.

When they were out of earshot, Wolfe asked, "Do you think they'll be able to try him for manslaughter?"

"Guaranteed," Garris said. "I contacted the investigators in Georgia. Since the time Dr. Stephenson made his accusations, they've compiled a fair amount of evidence proving Mr. Baltimore had been there but nothing to prove he'd purchased kerosene or flares."

"So how does his confession change anything if it's inadmissible?" Faith asked.

"It's the fact Mr. Baltimore identified the accelerant as kerosene. The police never released that detail," Chief Garris stated. "Even in his book, which otherwise contained a carbon copy description of the Georgia boat fire, Mr. Baltimore's character doused the boat with gasoline."

"Like Bill did," Faith said. "There were rags in the bottom of the boat. I could smell the gasoline on them when I pulled myself into the boat to untie Pierce."

"Pierce has a kerosene heater in his outdoor gazebo," Susan chimed in. "He likes to write out there even in the cold weather. And he always kept road flares in his car for emergencies."

"Good to know. With any luck, his lawyer will convince him the judge will go easier on him if Mr. Baltimore comes clean, which will also spare him from an unflattering trial." The chief motioned the rest of them in the direction from which he'd come. "Let's get you all back to the manor and dried off before we finish taking your statements."

Susan accompanied the chief on his ATV, and Eban said he'd walk, leaving the manor's ATV at Wolfe and Faith's disposal.

"Oh, wait," Faith said. "We're missing Watson."

As if on cue, Watson scampered through the trees dragging a baseball cap in his mouth. The sun caught something reflective on it, causing it to momentarily glint.

"That's unusual," Wolfe said. "Where did he find that?"

"It's the cap Bill was wearing. It must have fallen off when he was apprehended." Faith reached down and took it from Watson. "It has a reflective square sewn into the back."

She remembered what one of the retreat guests had said about the baseball cap on a figure lurking in the topiary garden the night Tara died. She showed the cap to Wolfe and reminded him of the woman's description.

"We'd better get this to the chief," Wolfe said.

They climbed onto the ATV. Faith sat behind Wolfe, trying hard not to drip all over him.

As soon as Watson leaped into her lap, Wolfe powered up the engine and sped off after the chief.

"The phone call I received before the police arrived was Midge. She said she found the smoking gun. She must have been talking about the needle used to kill Tara." Faith frowned at the reflective square on Bill's baseball cap, frustrated that she hadn't noticed it days ago. "And she'd been to Bill's B&B."

"Don't worry. He's not going anywhere anytime soon with a kidnapping and attempted murder charge hanging over his head."

"Oh no," Faith said when they cleared the trees near the manor.

A crowd had gathered around the police and Pierce and Bill.

Many held Pierce's newest book, apparently still hoping to score his autograph.

"Make way!" Officer Jan Rooney shouted, attempting to carve a path through the crowd for the officers escorting the men.

Cybil climbed atop the back of one of the empty ATVs to address the crowd. "If you love the stories in Pierce Baltimore's latest book, then you should be asking Susan Moore to autograph it. Pierce stole the stories from her." She smiled and motioned to Susan.

A collective gasp rose from the crowd, followed by exclamations of disbelief.

The officers took advantage of the diversion to hustle their suspects into the waiting squad cars.

Chuckling, Wolfe helped Faith from the ATV. "It looks as if Susan will get her fifteen minutes of fame even if she can't convince the courts she's the original author."

"She deserves it," Faith said.

Watson squirmed out of Faith's arms, then jumped to the ground and took off.

Eileen made a beeline to Faith and swept her into a warm hug. "I'm so glad you're okay."

Brooke followed suit and then Midge.

Faith showed them Bill's baseball cap and explained what she'd overheard.

"Is the guest who saw the figure lurking in the topiary garden out here?" Wolfe asked Faith.

She scanned the crowd and pointed the woman out to him.

Wolfe took the cap from Faith. "I'm going to show this to Garris."

"You should get out of those wet clothes," Eileen fussed.

Faith hesitated.

"It won't take long," Eileen pressed. "I'll let Chief Garris and Wolfe know you'll be right back."

Faith agreed and asked Midge to join her so she could fill Faith in on the smoking gun she'd discovered.

"I found the needle Bill used to kill Tara," Midge explained as they hurried to the cottage. "He tossed it into the trash at his B&B."

"I can't believe he would be so reckless," Faith remarked. "So how did you find it? Did you dig through all the garbage?"

"Thankfully, I didn't have to. The owner was shoveling the trash into a new bag when I got there, and I spotted the needle. If a raccoon hadn't tipped over the can and ripped apart the bags, the needle would have been buried under a ton of garbage at a transfer station by now."

"What a stroke of luck," Faith said. "Did anyone see Bill getting rid of it?"

"The B&B owner saw him throw it out."

"It's hard to believe that Bill wasn't more careful when he disposed of the needle."

Midge nodded. "I thought the same thing. And I asked why the owner didn't confront him. Apparently she got distracted by a phone call when it happened. She was worried that it could have injured the garbage collectors and was going to talk to Bill about it later but forgot. She was pretty upset over it."

"Did you give the needle to the police?"

"Yes, they're testing it for fingerprints and traces of sux."

Faith unlocked the front door of the cottage. "I can't believe Bill killed Tara. It's so senseless. He said she didn't even know who he was."

"He could have been lying so we wouldn't suspect him," Midge reasoned.

"True. I'll be right back." Faith went to her bedroom and changed into jeans and a sweater, then dragged a brush through her damp hair. As soon as she returned, she announced, "I'm ready. Let's go."

When they returned to the manor and rejoined their friends,

Faith was surprised to see two squad cars still there. They were empty. "Where are Pierce and Bill?"

"They were shivering like crazy," Eileen said, "so Officer Laddy took Pierce to his room to change into dry clothes. Bill had his suitcase in his truck, so Officer Tobin let him go inside to change too."

Faith glanced back to see Susan signing copies of the book Pierce had stolen from her, seemingly oblivious to her damp clothes, as Cybil looked on like a proud mother. "Well, it seems as if we've solved another case."

"Except for the bookcase incident," Brooke mused. "Cybil and Susan both deny having anything to do with it. Did you see Bill in the library that morning?"

"No." Faith frowned.

Nolan, who'd been standing nearby watching Susan, cleared his throat. "I can explain that mystery for you. I'm ashamed to admit I pulled the little prank."

Brooke stared at him in surprise.

Nolan snagged Faith's gaze, his own contrite. "I want to offer you my profound apology. I felt horrible when you took the brunt of its fall. I'd intended to confess when I invited you to join me for lunch, but you slipped away before I had the chance, and after that . . ." He shrugged. "The moment never seemed right."

"Apology accepted," Faith said.

Nolan clasped her hand gratefully. "Thank you."

Faith thought of something. "Can you clear up one other mystery? Who was that dark-haired man you were talking to in town the other day?"

"When I was in the flower shop, one of the other customers overheard me talking about the retreat with the clerk. It turned out the man was an aspiring novelist, so he stopped me on the sidewalk to pitch his story."

Faith nodded. "That must happen to you often."

"It's part of the job, I'm afraid." Nolan glanced back at Susan, who'd started toward the manor. "Now if you'll excuse me, I want to catch Susan before Cybil whisks her away. I'm going to offer to represent her. I imagine this weekend has given her plenty of fodder for a new book."

"That's terrific," Faith said. "I'm sure she'll appreciate your vote of confidence."

Nolan lowered his voice. "I hope she can forgive me for accusing her of plagiarizing Pierce's work. When he didn't show up to the book signing, Cybil filled me in on what was happening. But we'd expected the police to have Susan in handcuffs too."

"Until we had the chance to confront her about this morning's prank in Pierce's room, we weren't sure what else she might have been responsible for." Faith scanned the faces in the crowd. "I don't see Ruth. Has she heard the news?"

"Sort of," Midge said. "Before the chief headed out on the ATV, he told Marlene they might soon have the proof they needed to make an arrest in Tara's murder."

"Ruth all but fainted with relief when she heard that," Eileen added. "Marlene helped her back to her room to rest. She feared reporters might arrive and bombard her with questions too."

As the crowd dispersed, Chief Garris and Wolfe joined Faith and her friends.

"It seems you were right about the needle, Dr. Foster," Garris said. "I just got word the lab has confirmed it had traces of succinylcholine. And they were able to get several clean prints from it, so once we get Dr. Stephenson to the station and fingerprinted, we'll know if we have a slam dunk."

Officer Tobin escorted Bill out of the manor and toward one of the squad cars.

"I don't know why you're arresting me," Bill growled. "It's Baltimore who needs to pay for his crimes."

"Didn't you hear?" Midge chimed in. "The police found the needle you threw into your B&B's trash."

His face drained of color.

"And a witness spotted the distinctive reflective patch on the back of your baseball cap when you were lurking in the topiary garden that night," Faith added.

He shook his head. "It wasn't me. Lots of people wear caps like that."

Watson appeared, twining around Faith's legs, so Faith stooped to pick him up. He pawed insistently at Faith's cheek.

"What is it, Rumpy?"

Watson repeated the action, this time letting his claws scratch her ever so slightly.

She caught him by the paws to stop him. "That hurts."

Watson let out a strange, deep-throated meow, clearly trying to tell her something.

Faith glanced at Bill and noticed a scabbed-over scratch high on his cheek that traveled down beneath his growing whiskers. She spun toward Chief Garris. "Did the coroner find traces of human skin under Tara's fingernails?"

The chief looked from Faith to Bill and back to Faith. "Yes, several samples were sent to the state crime lab for DNA testing."

Faith turned back to Bill in triumph. "The real reason you stopped shaving was to hide the scratch Tara gave you when you stabbed her with the needle, wasn't it?"

"That's some imagination you've got there," he said, but she could see in his eyes that he was worried. "I am a vet after all. Scratches happen."

"DNA doesn't lie, and I suspect yours is what will incriminate you," Faith said. "What I don't get is why you did it. Unless you were also lying about Tara not recognizing you."

Finally, Bill snapped. "She knew what Pierce was, and she was letting him get away with it. She could have taken the story public, forced the police to investigate, but she refused. The second I saw her here and heard she wanted to be a novelist too, I knew all she cared about was what Pierce could do for her. She got what she deserved!"

Chief Garris motioned to Officer Tobin. "Get him out of here."

21

When Faith and Watson meandered up to the manor on Monday morning, the retreat guests had all checked out and the housekeeping staff had already taken down the creepy decorations.

"Feeling rested?" Wolfe asked, descending the grand staircase.

Faith smiled. "Yes, and I have to say it's nice to see the manor back to its serene state once more."

Marlene handed a clipboard to the staff member she'd been addressing and joined them in the middle of the lobby. "Our guests had seemed oddly thrilled by the whole turn of events—with their star writer being exposed as a murderous arsonist and plagiarizer."

"That's because they love horror," Faith replied. "They enjoy being scared out of their wits."

Wolfe grinned. "So I take it they didn't convert you to their taste in literature?"

"No. But I will admit that I now see some value in the horror genre beyond being a fix for adrenaline junkies."

Wolfe crossed his arms, his expression curious. "And what's that?"

"It forces us out of our complacency and shows us that we should always be on alert because even a tranquil setting like Castleton Manor is not necessarily as secure as it may appear."

Wolfe sighed. "Sadly true."

Brooke strolled over to them. "Well, don't get any ideas about suggesting a horror novel for next month's book club pick. I'd rather read a romance any day." She nudged Marlene with her elbow. "Wouldn't you?"

Marlene actually blushed. "Who doesn't enjoy a good romance?"

With a loud meow, Watson scampered across the lobby and

jumped onto an antique bureau displaying a selection of mysteries. The cat gently nudged a book in the middle of the display, tilting it forward from the rest, and then he leaped to the floor. He looked at them expectantly.

"I think Watson wants to offer a book suggestion." Wolfe strode to the bureau and picked up the novel Watson had chosen. With a chuckle, Wolfe held the cover of the book so they all could see it. "How appropriate. One of Lilian Jackson Braun's The Cat Who mysteries."

Brooke laughed. "It's like he knows we can't solve a mystery without him."

Watson sat and delicately washed a paw.

Faith rubbed his ears. "I wouldn't even try."

Up to this point, we've been doing all the writing. Now it's *your* turn!

Tell us what you think about this book, the characters, the bad guy, or anything else you'd like to share with us about this series. We can't wait to hear from *you*!

Log on to give us your feedback at:
https://www.surveymonkey.com/r/CastletonLibrary

Annie's FICTION